Ben Reed is stoned.
Ben Reed is armed.
Ben Reed is alone on the highway on his BMW and
Ben Reed is under surveillance.

A man sits in an office a thousand miles away from Ben Reed. He watches a screen. Ben Reed is a white dot on that screen. The man can kill Ben Reed by pushing a button on his desk. It will be legal.

Because Ben Reed is alone on the highway on his BMW. And because he's a longhair freak.

CenterForce
A novel of the near future

CenterForce

by T. A. WATERS

A Dell Book

for PAM
with much love

When a whole system is composed of a number
of systems, the one that tends to dominate
is the one that is *least* stable.

—*The Application of Cybernetics
to Psychiatry*

Published by
Dell Publishing Co., Inc.
1 Dag Hammarskjold Plaza
New York, New York 10017

This is a work of fiction—at time of publication.
Dell ® TM 681510, Dell Publishing Co., Inc.
Printed in the United States of America
First printing—December 1974

I

wei chi: before completion

He had had no desire, in June Utah evening, to have killed the man; and now that it was done, he had no desire to linger, to look at the body that was too still.

Across the pavement, blood, still moving slightly.

It trickled, following the slight camber of the roadway and a crack that had not been repaired, moving in a slow cautious stream until it touched the green scrub plant; it could neither nourish it nor overcome it, and it pooled around the base of the small plant.

There had been so many of them; if they had been on motorcycles as Ben had been, they would have killed him certainly. But they had used pickup trucks and jeeps, and had not been able to follow along the dry arroyo. Except for the man who had been on horseback; who had had something going in his mind out of the old west; who had been ambitious; who had paid for his ambition the way Caesar had.

. . . who had been ripped apart by the twelve-gauge slug, his unused Colt Woodsman flung convulsively twenty feet to the side as his body had spun with the impact, spun and fallen to the too-stillness.

. . . who had held, with the men in the jeeps and the trucks the *let's get that fucking freak, that longhair bastard on the cycle* thought, the desire to death that had brought him death.

No desire to linger; but Ben waited, now, for the sound of motors, hooves, the sea-like crackle of a sweepbeam from a laser truck. He knew that they had

no GEMs, for he would have heard easily the sound
of the twin downward-mounted props; and because
they would have ridden their air bubble above the
arroyo, to where he was, and would have made him
dead.

He thought about that, now too, and realized that in
thinking he was affirming that he wasn't dead. Sometimes it was the only way you knew that you were . . .
that you were.

The scrub plant moved, slightly, in a quick low
breeze across the blackened and cracked roadway,
from a napalm grenade, he thought vaguely; the blood
at the base of the plant had stopped pooling, was still
like its source.

And no sound not of a place without people.

Absently, without his particular volition, the forefinger of his left hand moved around the front bar of
the trigger guard and pushed on the lateral safety. The
hands, waldos of the brain, lowered the Winchester.
The feet, in their turn, moved Ben to the bike, and he
sat down on the worn black saddle and shuddered so
heavily that he was startled by the sound.

Ben Reed:

now a unit

now a thing of a piece

now having lasted three decades and some

sat in the Utah darkness alone except for the invisible animals in the brush; and the man he had killed;
and the gunblue and blackleather cycle.

alone; where now was the only time there was.

II

ta chuang: power of the great

(EXTRACT FROM CORRO MANUSCRIPTS/FRAG. 81a)
. . . continent. Few could have imagined that the pattern, even with the aid of a pendulum effect stemming from the early years of the disturbances, would set into a permanent mode of existence.

First intimations of the situation to come were the series of Police Strikes. Forces of law and order in the large urban centers had become paramilitary in nature, fairly describable as mercenary armies, and were well paid and equipped.

Smaller cities and towns, however, could not meet this expense, and fell victim to the sociopathic element driven from the large urban areas. One must be fair in this analysis; in a significant percentage of the conflicts the violence was initiated by the towndwellers, either in fear or in prejudice.

Whatever the seminal factors, there was great bloodshed, and many were the acts of hatred and vengeance. The police forces in these areas simply disappeared; law-enforcement officers, unprotected as they were, generally were shot on sight, and to take such a job was considered suicidal.

The government, rebuilt in New York City after the destruction of Washington in the election riot of 1976, employed within the framework of martial law the infamous stricture which came to be known as the Domestic Enemies Act . . .

III

lu: the wanderer

There was the comforting screech of the wheelie as he shot up the access ramp toward the thruway. The back wheel, too, left the ground as he crested, and Ben shifted his body weight forward so that both wheels made contact with the road simultaneously; opening the throttle then, sensing the dial panel rather than seeing it, he geared up with a fine and metal-synapse-subconscious rhythm.

press down
hook up
up
up . . .

. . . it was five hundred and ninety cubic centimeters of force. Much of it had been born at the Bavarian Motor Works some years before, in 1971; in the embrace of Ben's legs, it did not seem to care that the road, cracked and treacherous, whipped beneath it at a mile-and-a-half a minute.

It did not care because Ben loved and trusted it; it had saved his life, had done things motorcycles were not supposed to be able to do. In Omaha, during the bad year, it had dropped thirty feet into a gravel pit but still, miraculously, had taken him out . . .

. . . across the river in Texas: an AR-15 slug half into the gearbox and Ben only half-conscious, it had taken him away to safety, accepting the fumbling, instinctual orders from the crazed man astride it and *knowing*, knowing it must save him.

He knew its nuts and bolts, its engine-heart, frame

and wheels as a man knows the body of his loved one—
with warm familiarity, with watchful concern.

It was his family; wife mother son. He would have
killed to protect it from hurt and from pain.

He had.

Now blue dusk. He shot like an invisible arrow
toward a corner of Utah, on a hard blackline across
nothing. Ben rode without lights; the moon was full
and the sky was clear, and his night vision was excellent. Had it not been he would not have dared to
ride. To use a beam on any negotiable road, particularly now that the vigilantes had sent a bulletin to the
CenterForce Patrols, would be to make himself a target.

For the laser if you were lucky: brightness and
nothing.

For the mace-mines if you weren't. The mace-mines
meant, unless you could kill yourself, that they'd have
you. Then a little

   snick snick

in the front of your brain and another little

   snick snick

around your balls and then no one would have you.
And maybe it wouldn't matter except—

   —they said you remembered.

IV

shih ho: biting through

*Statement of James Handelin, AKA Sparky Jim/
/onboard CenterForce Patroller J4413/ /SW Sector
Eight/ /*
(in response to interrogation; edited)

Not a way of life.

You hear that shit all the time. Not a way of life.
Fuck, man, do this; smash your radios, your 3Vs. Don't
talk to anybody, don't go out on the street. Man, don't
think.

We'll still be there. We're not made out of dreams,
can you dig it? The knives are real and the blood is real
and we die too, just like you see on the veecasts when-
ever you shits are lucky enough to get one of us. We're
real, baby; try us off your fender at ninety, maybe, and
then you'll really shit because you'll know that if we're
real enough to die, the way we do when you get a
chance, then we're real enough to kill you, to cut
through your marshmallow outside to where the pain
nerves are and make you feel life.

Feel life?

Straight, mother, because you only feel life when it's
part of something. Like: sugar *is* because there's lemon;
fucking *is*, because there's being lonely; life *is*, because
there's death; pain in the guts *is*, because there's giving
some other cat pain in the guts.

Yin-yang. Can you dig it?

So there you are, baby, canned in your urbs, and
here we are, out in growly-monster land. Yin-yang.
Must be something else to watchbird watchyou watch

it—the three-vee—hear those New York cats say that we ain't really here. Like maybe it's gray fog out here or something and we're just a superstition. Seems like you spend a lot of bread on superstition; lot of you cats with those funny CenterForce helmets got spent too, right?

But it's cool with us if you want to keep playing pretend. Another ten years, you dumb shits, and we'll have enough manpower to take you all down, or did you think that the little chicks that keep splitting from the urbs come out here just to wash our socks?

And it's happening, man, just like everything else happened that wasn't supposed to, and it don't matter a shit that you got CenterForce guns and CenterForce buses and all that crap.

The age of magic is over, at least your kind of magic. We're the ones got the warlocks now, baby.

(ADDITIONAL: Prisoner Handelin was DOA Sector Eight/CenterForce HQ/ /died as result of injuries sustained during arrest procedure/ /age 23: no previous record/ /)

V

kou: coming to meet

There is a crown
but it's not in a town
and you can't shine it up for your glory
There is a throne
but it's not made of stone
and it's not in a fairy-tale story
Your crown is the stars
capped with crimson from Mars
and your throne is the land and the sea
Your kingdom is love
and the blue sky above
and in knowing that here you are free . . .

—*from a rock song, circa 1976*

VI

chien: obstruction

The road swung, as if it had nothing better to do, through canyons lined with rock towers. Ben's eyes flicked from the almost invisible road surface to the dark places and summits of the minicrags. An ambush was unlikely, this far off the beaten track but . . .

. . . stranger things had happened. CenterForce had its share of fanatics. He was happier when the sides of the highway opened up again and he could see the country. A culvert overpass appeared about three-quarters of a mile up the monotony; Ben geared down as he approached. It would be as good a place as any.

He braked and skidded across the shoulder to the grassy lip that sloped down to the stream. Beautiful; the culvert pipe was ten feet high, and the stream was only a trickle. Ben urged the bike down the slope.

For a split-instant as he descended there was a brilliant flash of light. For a moment Ben was unsure what had happened; then he realized it was the sodium-arc searchbeam from a CenterForce Patroller.

■ *Jesus! Did they see me?* ■

He killed the engine and coasted into the culvert. Up the opposite wall slightly, and back, now, onto the kickstand in one motion and off, the Winchester out of the saddle-sheath before the cycle had settled, and scrambled up to the culvert lip . . .

The cyclop-beam glared at him. Ben judged the bus was still a quarter-mile away; in any case, close enough, for the beam had veered from the faded centerline of the road to the side, and now probed the edges of the culvert. He had been seen; he was fair game.

And the game was on; accepted knowledge of both
    sides.

They would capture and/or kill him
        or

he would (allowed only the single option) kill them.

The vigilantes had not wasted any time getting in touch with the CenterForce dispatcher, thought Ben, as he pumped a slug into the firing chamber of the twelve-gauge. As he sighted on the approaching bus something flashed vaguely in his mind, someone years ago describing the simple version of the laws of thermodynamics—*you can't win, you can't break even, you can't get out of the game*—yes: here was a game from which there was no escape, which would result in a local increase in entropy. Which would result in death.

First move, and first things first. Ben took a deep breath, exhaled slightly, and then held his air for a moment as he squeezed off the slug. The sound of the tire exploding was the first of many echoes to the blast of the shotgun.

The CenterForce driver had not been prudent; the bus was still traveling at over fifty miles an hour when its right front tire disintegrated. The huge bus heeled over in slow motion with no loss of forward speed, pointed impossibly into the air for a hundred feet or more and then, roof shooting sparks as it touched the road surface, the bus skidded over the shoulder. It rolled over onto one side and stopped.

Its forward somersault had turned the bus completely around; there were several seconds of absolute and unnatural silence, the silence you would only hear in desert country after such alien din as this. Suddenly the rear hatch-locks, which had been fitted with explosive bolts, were blown off and the double doors swung open.

There was a low whine of electric motors from within,

and then something glinted lunar blue, an apostrophe in the black rectangle.

Ben was familiar with CenterForce armament regs, and he knew what the apostrophe punctuated, what was pointing at him. The device was a modification of an old fighter-interceptor machinegun; it could fire two hundred and fifty explosive rounds per second.

A small fraction with large implications; it would only take 1/250th of a second's worth of death to be quite enough death for Ben.

And his second's worth passed over his head; the dirt shoulder on the other side of the culvert exploded along a ten-foot length, and he was showered with dirt and gravel. They would wait, now, for twenty seconds or more; and then would come the Mace grenades. Fifteen seconds . . .

. . . but there was always the Patroller's gas tank, and Ben knew where that was. He had moved silently along the culvert to several yards' distance from his original position, and now looked at the side of the huge bus from an angle; his eyes letting his brain superimpose an x-ray picture of its interior.

The tank would be

(another shell in the chamber)

about

(finger tightening against trigger; mover of the scythe)

there.

■■■■■■■■■■■

No contest, he decided a few minutes later, watching the burning and twisted thing (nausea on the wind) (black, oily smoke), and waiting to see that the fire did not spread.

But perhaps they didn't care how many it had taken or would take; perhaps they weren't counting anymore.

VII

sun: the gentle

Momma love,

Marc said I should write you—I'll tell you about him—but I would have done it anyway so you wouldn't worry.

I guess maybe you hate me or think I don't care about you or Daddy anymore, but I tried to explain in the note I left. It was like I was pretending all the time, and I'm too old to keep pretending. Sixteen is a lot older than it was when you were that age.

Anyway, I didn't run away with some boy or anything like that. I went to live with some friends in this ashram (that means kind of like a religious community) and they've all been very nice, and nothing's happened to me—you know what I mean. It's a long way from Columbus, it's not even in Ohio, so there isn't any use in you trying to find me and I wish you wouldn't. You were always saying about how much trouble I was anyway and now I'm not. I'm taking care of myself and nobody lies to me anymore.

Marc said I should write XXXX (I said that before), and he's a very beautiful person. He's kind of old, I guess he must be nearly thirty-five, but he's really aware of all of us and we can tell him our problems and he'll tell us what the right thing to do would be. But he's just a friend. I haven't had much time to get to meet some of the boys here anyway because I have to help Sara with the nursery and taking care of all those babies is a full time job. I'm usually too tired to do much of anything at the end of the day.

We have dances sometimes in the evening and they're kind of fun, but the best part of being here is just being able to talk to people and not have to worry about putting up a front or a big show for them. I have more friends now that I really care about than I had in my whole life up to the time I came here—and I've found out that people really can fool you sometimes. I've been able to think about people I knew and the things they did, and I've realized that they really weren't my friends at all. It's like I just woke up after sleep-walking all my life.

I'm learning to play the guitar and read music but I'm not very good at it yet.

You don't have to worry about my clothes. It's warm here most of the time and Joan and Sara gave me some things and helped me make some new things of my own. You can give whatever I left to Lorraine or Cissy if you want to, because I don't need them here and I don't think I'll ever wear that kind of clothes again. They seem kind of silly now, but I guess that Cissy or Lorraine would like them.

Please don't worry about me. Really, I'm safer here than I was in the city, and everybody takes care of each other. There aren't any fights because everybody looks up to Marc and they'd be ashamed to try to explain why if they ever started fighting, and if you do something wrong here you *have* to explain to Marc and everybody why you did it.

I still love you and Daddy very much. I'd send my address but I know Daddy would give it to CenterForce and then they would come out here to get me and probably hurt a lot of people if anyone tried to help me. But please don't worry! I'll be all right and some-time I'll come back to visit or something. I'll send you cards so you'll know I'm okay.

Lisa says some people passing through are going to New York and they can mail the letter for me there. I'm going to give it to them and cross my fingers that it doesn't get lost.

I just read over the letter and noticed that I said at the beginning that maybe you hate me; I hope that's not true and that you understand that my leaving had nothing to do with wanting to hurt you. I just have to do what I'm doing because I have to live my life. Please understand and love me; I still love you and Daddy very-very much.

JILL

P.S. Tell Daddy not to bother Andy Marion because he doesn't know where I am either. I don't even know if he knows I'm gone.

VIII

ting: the caldron

You have your choice; you can move during the day,
and be able to see the highway and avoid some of the
worst patches and stretches. If you do that, CenterForce
will see you, and between the copter and the GEM give
you a very hard time, perhaps the hardest time of all.
Or:

Or you can move at night, keeping down to about
thirty if you want any chance at all when the road
drops from under your bike, and hope you can make
it from one enclave to the next whistling along the
dark. Be in the wrong place when the sun comes up
and you don't see it hit noon; they aren't supposed to
shoot on sight but there's a lot of things they're not
supposed to do.

If you're really going to try to make it, you have to
have a motor, and it has to be on two wheels. Our
information is that nobody's made it from Missouri to
the Pacific in a car, except one cat in a Land Rover.
CenterFuzz have the highway routes sewed up, and if
you plan to do any traveling that's a fact you had better
face now.

Also dig that you can't count on any help from
straights; we've met some beautiful people in un-
expected places, but depending on finding that kind of
help could leave you in a very down situation. What
this means is: spare gas tank, always kept full; parts for
maintenance, and if you can't fix it don't travel on it;
water tablets, uppers, and a little something to eat
that'll keep.

A lot of brothers and sisters have taken to fucking over the CenterFuzz, running a lot of little violence numbers. *We* don't think this is going to produce anything but more heat, and those of you who remember the Nebraska thing might recall that it started with just this same kind of crap.

Along with this goes another thing: if you've got CenterFuzz on you, *for whatever reason*, don't bring it into one of the enclaves. As a general rule they've been letting us alone, but the SeaBear installation at Monterey was burned to the ground because of *one cat* trying to shake the heat; they got him, and twenty-eight other people besides, just for laughs. Just remember that as individuals we're none of us worth destroying a whole group.

Try to manage some sort of medical checkup before you start moving; passing around VD, or hepatitis for that matter, may not be the best way of repaying people for being hospitable, and for sometimes taking considerable risks.

If you're on the East Coast right now, you may have heard that here at StarChild we're supposed to be very hostile and uptight; we don't think so. What we *know*, is that we're in the middle of Arizona, we've got one major water supply and not much land for farming, and if they come down heavy our only way out is down into the Mexican desert, which is the same as no way out; and we have survived. StarChild has lasted for eight years, and that's partly because we figure we've got something to protect, which means that we don't let you in just because you may look freaky—and partly because we all pull our own weight. It may not be a free ride, but it's been a pretty good one so far.

The key and the purpose is to *survive*; remember, they can't live forever.

—Marc Hammond, *StarChild Bulletin Number Eighty*: Overland

IX

lin: approach

Wheel turning behind wheel turning; the blackened seamed roadway, beneath and beneath and beneath. The wheels with their gyroscopic function, Ben thought he could fall asleep and it would go on: the horse knows the way.

But perhaps they weren't gyroscopes at all; maybe they were the engines of God, the prayer wheels, every spin every revolution sending a thousand supplications up to Heaven from strips of parchment. He could make a hollow axle and stuff it with the little paper-prayers out of a god-fortune-cookie; what would he write, what could he ask God for?

No; terrible things would happen, because he would say the wrong things on the little pieces of paper. Every three feet he traveled, each revolution of the wheel, other dozens of imprecations straggling to the face of God. After a while God would get tired and smack him.

■■■■■■■■■ the chemical was an alkaloid; sixty-five milligrams of it were having a fine time in him. *Psilocybe mexicana* had traveled from Guadalajara to Oakland to Boston to Salt Lake City, from a pile of cow shit in a field that someone must have looked at closely, to Ben Reed's circulatory system. Enough of it, which was a lot more, could kill him; this much could only watch him kill himself, and that might happen ■■■■■■■■■

God probably wouldn't come himself, Ben decided, and his eyes moistened at the realization. *I don't even matter to God, then who . . . ?* Hm. God is on the side of the big battalions; how many divisions has the Pope? And the equation popped into his head: *God is on the side of CenterForce; CenterForce can't catch me;* ergo, *God can't catch me.* Immediate plans for the act of defiance now made safe; how big a hole could he drill in the axle for the pieces of prayer?

New inspiration. Stuff them into the tire itself. Enough of them and he wouldn't even have to worry about flats, he could roll along forever on his curses to God.

He flashed on Amy, talking miles and hours back in the place outside (Denver?) some town. "I wish to Christ you hadn't given him that," she was saying to Gretsch not to Ben, "you know he's not going to take it here and have something nice. He'll wait until he gets out there and has half the world after him and that's when he'll decide to drop."

"What better time?" Between pot-giggles. "I'm on a death trip, right?"

Amy had looked at him with puzzled contempt. "I don't know *what* kind of a trip you're on. I'll tell you this, though, it doesn't seem to have much to do with other people. You've got all the emotional giving of a starfish."

Gretsch, behind the cable-spool table, looked up from the compartmented plastic box that had one of every kind of pill in the world. He glanced at Ben. "This is not the Amy that we all know and some of us love, my boy. You must be something of an inspiration to her." He turned to Amy. "Anyway, you should be a bit more temperate in your metaphors. It is obvious that you have never felt the sucking of a starfish."

Amy was taking a hit. "Still holds," she said in a breathless voice, tightwire strained; exhaled. "With a starfish you only let him eat as much of you as you like," she continued in normal tones. "Let this one get one bit and he'll devour you and thank your memory for the meal."

"That almost sounds like an invitation," observed someone in a corner of the room.

"Get fucked," Amy said sweetly to the ceiling.

"Now," said Gretsch, "that *does* sound like an invitation."

More clicky pot-giggles; Amy the last laugh, and it came out under cover of the blue-tinted smoke and quickly disguised itself as a cough. "Dammit," she said between giggle-coughs, "you made me lose it," referring to the escaping smoke; and fell over the cushions onto Ben. Levi-leg against Levi-leg, breasts under the jersey against his stomach, she looked up at him. *I will have you now, starfish,* she did not say, *we will see who is the greater devourer.*

It was an awfully small room in the back of Gretsch's house, with one window above a wide shelf; so small that the edges of the mattress turned up at each wall, as though the room was in the process of being padded for the convenience of Gretsch's friends. *Particularly me,* Ben was thinking when Amy seemed to read his mind and explained that it had been a closet.

Bump, bump. Elbows and feet knocking on the walls as they got undressed, not wanting to touch each other at all until there was all to touch.

Amy, "Yes. Now," hands guiding, pulling; he was going to lie down beside her, but she moved him down on her, a small hand leading him into her as lip met lip, the thrust of her tongue and his body in perfect relationship of hunger and joy. They both sighed, and laughed at the coincidence; her legs wrapping his, her hand behind his neck, his hand cupping a breast too hard but receiving no protest.

▯▯▯▯▯▯▯▯▯▯▯
that's when he'll decide to drop
▯▯▯▯▯▯▯▯▯▯▯

His hands were wet in the gloves; the needle glowed palely on 70; there was a bridge behind him that he must have gone over, and he had an erection.

■ ■ ■ ■ ■ ■ ■ ■ ■   the *Psilocybe mexicana* was being absorbed; the effects had peaked, and begun to dis-
sipate, when the mind's fantasies dictated an increase
in circulation. *Psilocybe* had another chance to produce
death or magic ■ ■ ■ ■ ■ ■ ■ ■ ■ ■

Ben's right foot began the shift-down process before
his mind had made any decision, working along the
lines of a conspiracy it had formed with the clutch-hand.
As its heart began to calm the BMW moved stolidly
across the gravel shoulder and down along the fenced-
in brush. After a few seconds the fence gave up; the
cycle arced around the terminating post and back
amongst the trees.

   . . . he was on the ground, leaning against the tree,
as was the BMW; the curtain of leaves was Amy reach-
ing down, naked as night . . .

   . . . his body floated toward her and toward release . . .

X

wu wang: innocence

If Marc had been there, she thought, it wouldn't have happened. Marc would have seen to it that the bikers didn't get into StarChild to begin with; he would have protected her, like—like the people she didn't have anymore.

Arizona afternoon; sunlight slantwise through red-brick dust, a lazy warmth of the kind that was never noticed, and no breath of wind. Quiet; the paused silence for a time, before the preparations for dinner were begun. Children unseen but distantly heard as they played in the dry arroyo; a mother pausing at the door of a quonset hut, another near a geodesic dome, in a brief concerned pause until they picked the happy shouts of their own children out of the distant gabble.

Quiet; a moment to be with one's mate, a head against a shoulder and fingers through the hair; firm softness of the aged mattress, pressure of one body against another; the alchemy of nature turning love to passion.

Quiet; shattered, broken.

Jimmie had seen them, down at the gate. They had hit him, had broken the walkie-talkie; Jimmie had still tried to warn Marc and the others, a part of his mind screaming that Marc was not there, that it wouldn't make any difference because there was no way he could get there before the cycles.

It had made no difference; he was so confused by the beating that he had wandered the wrong way. After a time he found himself out at the highway, laboriously figured out what he had been doing, and cried.

Everyone inside the main perimeter knew something was wrong as soon as they heard the motors; there were too many of them. As the sound of the engines grew, all other sounds of StarChild faded and died before their onslaught.

Jill had seen the dust cloud of their approach, had known something was wrong, for a few minutes before they arrived; she had done nothing, for in her there was no fear. They were bad, maybe, but they wouldn't hurt *her*; why, they would have no reason to hurt her.

The possibility of doom roared to a stop in the center of the complex; engines were lion-roar gunned, and quelled to silence. For a time, then, there was a metallic quiet, punctuated only by the snapping of a tent flap, whipping in the low urgent wind.

And Marc was—in Scottsdale?—Marc was away, only for a few hours it had been understood; there was no one to talk to the bikers, to find out what they wanted. Jill stood beside the low bulk of the electric pump; she stood quietly, still not afraid. (She wondered if soon she would begin to feel the fear; it was like a wet electricity all about her, an unverbalized contagion that might sweep over her at any moment. If the others were afraid, it must be for good reason, then—and she did not let herself complete the thought.)

Hey, catch the blonde action.
You fucking crazy man, ain't enough meat on her.
Enough for me. I could eat that right up.
Fucking cradle robber.
Better the cradle than the grave, mother.
Dig Sonny: won't know whether to fuck her or adopt her.
Going to teach her everything, right, Sonny?

*Teach her more than you'll ever know, that's for damn
    sure.*

They were talking about her? They were talking about
her; so strange, she thought—they didn't even know her.
She was wise enough to know what strategy would
dictate; pretend you had not heard, go into one of the
tents or domes as though you just wanted to get something and would be right back out—and then go out the
back way, back through the scrub and the cactus, down
the slope to the gully. Out to the highway and

And then where? Even if she could make it to
Marble Fork, there were cyclists there too; someone
said they were running the town now, and Gaines, who
had been the Sheriff, didn't do a thing anymore.

In the other direction, Los Caballos; no one there
who would help, even if she could make it that far.

The voices had not stopped, but the dialogue was
playing to its necessary end: *think I'll check that stuff
out.*

It was the one they had called Sonny who swung his
legs from the motorcycle and walked through the
powdery tan dust toward her.

Jill could only think, at that moment, that he had
never stopped grinning.

XI

chieh: limitation

FADE IN:

Day—Country Road—Long Shot

We are looking down from a HIGH ANGLE to a featureless country road, badly paved. There is a stand of trees to one side of the road, and as camera SLOW ZOOMS in we are able to make out a parked motorcycle and a SLEEPING FIGURE beside it.

CUT TO:

Day—Stand of Trees—C.U.

At ground level, we see the face of BEN REED through the waving tall grass; it is an Aztec prince's face—high cheekbones, deepset eyes, black hair above a high forehead. As we watch, his eyes flick open; there is no trace of sleepiness in them. He hears something, and now we hear it too—the sound of a CenterForce Patrol bus, we learn, as we

CUT TO:

Day—Road—Long Shot

The bus, windshield glinting in the sunlight, moves slowly along the road toward the camera.

CUT TO:

Day—Motorcycle—C.U.

Ben's hands appear on the cycle seat and handlebar as he pulls the cycle down to lie flat, revealing his face. His expression does not show fear, only resentment.

      Ben

      Mother fucker.

CUT TO:

Day—Interior of Bus Cab—M.C.U.

We are looking out at the road ahead, over the heads of DRIVER #1 and DRIVER #2, who sit at dual controls much like those in aircraft. Between them are three TV screens; one shows a telescopic view of the road ahead, the second shows the view from the rear of the bus, and the third is a computer-display map with a dot of light moving along it. For several seconds nothing seems to be happening, then we hear

> Voice (over)
> Getting a ding.

Driver #2 picks up what appears to be a wireless microphone from a magnetic clip beside him.

> DRIVER #2
> Put it on readout.

A small white circle with a cross inside it appears on the readout screen. The readout should remind us enough of the opening shot that we know it is Ben's cycle being indicated on the screen.

> DRIVER #2
> Got it. Visual scan.

His hand moves to a switch console.

CUT TO:

Forward View TV Screen—C.U.—Matte

The BUS CAMERA point of view swings from the road ahead to the side, PANNING with the bus's forward motion until it reaches the stand of trees. It ZOOMS IN on the trees, keeping them in the frame, and does SLOW PAN across them.

CUT TO:

Driver #2—Angle—E.C.U.

He is studying the screen.

> Voice of Driver #1 (over)
> Anything?
> Driver #2
> No.
> Voice of Driver #1 (over)
> Want me to pull in?

CUT TO:

Day—Ben Reed—E.C.U.

Looking over the back of his head, we see the Patrol bus moving across his line of vision on the road.

> Voice of Driver #2 (over)
>> No. Probably just a septic tank. It doesn't take much to trip that detector.

CUT TO:

Day—Ben Reed—E.C.U.

We hold on his face for several seconds as his eyes follow the bus out of sight. We DOLLY BACK as he finally stands up. On his face for a moment a smile flickers. Then he pulls the cycle upright.

CUT TO:

Kick Starter of Cycle—C.U.

Ben's boot slams the starter down and the engine roars into life. We hear the sound of revving for a moment, and then the cycle moves out of frame. We HOLD on the crushed grass where the cycle has passed; as the sound of the engine fades in the distance, the blades of grass begin slowly to rise again.

FADE OUT

XII

ken: keeping still

AGENT: Jonathan Gansell/S14 B2a
LOCATION: Marble Fork, Arizona
DATE: (deleted)
COVER OPERATION/PROCEDURE: (deleted)
REPORT NO.: 42
TEXT: Since the deposing of Eddy (Edward) Gaines from his position as Sheriff by the townspeople, in favor of Grogan's motorcyclists, there have been no major changes. Gaines continues to try to harass the cyclists in various ways; as noted in report #4, he owns Marble Fork's only beer parlor, a gathering place for Grogan and his people. In recent weeks there have been a number of incidents at the bar between its staff and the customers.

Terry Grogan continues to exercise iron control over his group; since his murder of Joseph (Curly) Michaels, he has been undisputed as leader.

Grogan appears to take his peace-keeping duties very seriously, and is gradually trying to make over his disorganized gang into a romanticized conception of the military. In some instances he has carried this conception to considerable lengths, as the following will indicate:

On (date deleted), while Grogan was busy with his mistress Trina Gordon (see report #28), it was decided by a number of cyclists to take a run to StarChild, the ashram a few miles west of Marble Fork. Shortly thereafter Grogan learned of their absence and set out in pursuit, accompanied by a number of other cyclists including myself.

We arrived to find that little had as yet taken place, except for the beating of a StarChild perimeter guard; one of the errant cyclists, identified only as Sonny, was about to attempt the rape of an underage female inhabitant of the ashram. Grogan killed the man with a karate chop to the neck. Apologizing to the girl and to the other members of the ashram, he then departed.

Disciplinary action is planned by Grogan for the surviving cyclists, but thus far he has not revealed to anyone just what form that action will take. His severe reprisal against Sonny does not seem to have weakened his position of leadership in any way; indeed, it seems to have been strengthened.

Further investigation of Dr. Michelson (report #16) does not support the hypothesis advanced by HQ Advisory that he is supplying the inhabitants of the ashram with psychedelics. His own moral stance, while not violently opposed to the use of such drugs, would seem to preclude providing them or fostering their use, and there is no evidence from my source at the ashram that he has done so.

It may be further commented that except for the use of such legal items as red wine and marijuana, moodchangers are little employed at the ashram. The focus is rather on a quasi-oriental meditative experience.

Political orientation/involvement at StarChild continues to be nil. Except for a desire to be left to themselves, inhabitants of the ashram have little thought of the outside world. Such documents as they publish (enclosure #A), though certainly not in concert with Federal aims, display no open opposition; there is indicated a predisposition not to accept fugitives from CenterForce and other Federal peace-keeping agencies.

Political orientation of Grogan and his cyclists remains in general alignment with that of controlling agencies; Grogan's new-found military mystique (see above) may bring his actions and procedures into even closer concert with the desires of Federal government.

Possible point of friction to be noted: unconfirmed reports indicate that Marriette Gaines, daughter of the erstwhile Sheriff, may have moved to StarChild. If this has happened, Gaines could react in unpredictable and troublesome ways. Request hereby made to HQ Advisory for Analysis and Policy statement with, if it appears necessary, a Special Authorization.

Analysis and Policy also requested on Marriette Gaines (enclosure #B), regarding possible removal from ashram, either overtly or through secondary procedures.

There are no indications at present of security breaks or flaws in cover; agent therefore requests that HQ Advisory hold in abeyance suggested assignment of secondary to this area. In event of any major change, personnel could be obtained by this agent from Albuquerque Central or the New Phoenix installation.

TRANSMITTAL: CODELEX/COMSAT 22/IAA PRIORITY

XIII

ming i: darkening of the light

Before we start this there's one thing that you have to understand. I really don't think these cards predict the future. They—

Well, just wait a minute and I'll tell you.

I don't think they predict the future, or that they're acausal phenomena; what Jung called synchronicity. What that means is just that there may be two things that happen at the same time—well, like a person's life and a tarot reading, or the position of the stars—and maybe they're not connected, these two things, but there are still patterns between them.

But I don't think they work that way. I think that every event in your life influences the events that come after, and anything that happens, even a reading, is an event, right? So what that means is that the very act of my reading the cards for you could have some influence on the rest of your life. More than it should if you take it seriously, and if you don't there isn't much point in my doing it, is there?

What?

Because you asked me to and you're a pretty boy who fucks nice.

No, I shuffle them; you just cut them, in three piles, right to left, like that.

This first one is the Significator; it represents you. Mm-mmn. Let me lay them all out first.

Well, that's interesting; looks like somebody's going to get you. No, not at all; in a very nice way—just like I got you, I think. Look:

You: *The Chariot.*
What crosses you: *King of Pentacles.*
What is above: *Page of Cups.*
What is below: *Nine of Swords.*
What is behind: *Eight of Swords.*
What is before: *Queen of Pentacles.*
Yourself: *Two of Wands*
Your House: *Eight of Cups*
Your Influence: *Three of Swords*
Your Goal: *The World*

No, it doesn't mean that you're going to get the world—anyway not like you think it means. Just let me look at them for a while. You see, it's all in the patterns; no particular card has a specific meaning.

You've been going through a long period of conflict, and I don't mean just with CenterFuzz and people like that. The conflict has been mostly inside you. It—

Ben, you don't have to impress me; I am already very impressed. There are things about you that I like a lot. Now I can read the cards for you *really*—the cards that are there—or I can just say a lot of things that will sound nice and make you feel good, for a while, anyway. But even if I don't tell you what I see, I've already seen it, so it doesn't make that much difference. And I'm not asking you to agree with everything I say; just consider it.

You're a Pisces, aren't you? It's very much part of the pattern here. The impression I get is that you've been going through life for quite a long time now as though you were acting a role. You do things, and you think you enjoy them, but when you're honest with yourself you realize that a lot of what you're doing just doesn't make sense.

You've been Skinnering for most of—oh, that means that you haven't really initiated much, if anything; you've just been letting circumstance dictate pretty much everything you do. That has a couple of advantages; you don't have to introspect much about your life, and you don't really have to take responsibility for the things that happen to you, the things you do.

Oh, sit down, Ben—I thought you realized that I'm not trying to criticize you. Whatever I say you can forget about as soon as you leave, if you want to. I should think you would want to hear the rest of it, anyway, to see if there was anything you consider good in it.

Besides, that wasn't a criticism peculiar to you; most of us Skinner, most of the time.

You seem to have been involved in a lot of violence, a lot of death, and it isn't real to you. You don't let it be real because if it was, then you'd have to sit down somewhere and decide whether you and the people who died were victims of circumstance or whether you had options.

There's some sort of knowledge somewhere, some sort of secret key to everything that's happening—from time to time you wonder about it; whether if you could find it the universe would suddenly make sense. But at the same time you know that you aren't going to search for it, and you don't know quite why.

You'll like this part. There are two women—actually, a woman and a girl. You're going to travel for a while longer, and then circumstances will Skinner you right to a stop where the woman is; she has a lot of power, there's death and heaviness about her, lines like a web of emotion, she—she'll be very dangerous to you. The girl is just the opposite; she will need you desperately, and you may wonder when it happens why you should help her, for it won't seem that there is much to gain—and I can't tell what you will do. I can only tell you that one of them is life and one of them is death, and I don't know which is which.

When you get to that point you will have to come alive, if you haven't before then; you'll have to make a conscious choice; even if it's the wrong one, you just can't give your life away by default.

Ben, you've got to realize who you really are, not who you want people to think you are. Pisces people do that a lot, and you've really got it bad, because what you are and what you seem to be—what you want *me* to think you are, even—they're two different people, and I don't think they will like each other much when they finally meet.

Oh, dammit, wait!

There's the loyalty thing, the trust—somebody you trust will try to hurt you; you've got to—

Ben. Oh, Ben; you just can't wait to meet it, can you?

XIV

chung fu: inner truth

We exist in two worlds,
    the inner and the outer.
The inner world is that of the mind and spirit.
The outer world is that of external reality.
All conflicts are between
    the inner and outer worlds;
    yet, all we know of the outer world
    are the impressions of its existence
    received by the inner.
Are then these conflicts real—
    or are they but the phantoms
    of our quarrelsome minds?
    If they are real, how can we know this?
If they are illusion, how can we know this?
The search for truth is the search for *consistency*;
    for an identity of form and content
    in the two worlds.
Only that which exists in both worlds—
    in the single outer world and in
    all the inner worlds
    of all people
    can be said to partake of reality.
Inner truth
    when it is that only
    is the truth of the spirit.
It can be as real as iron or fire
    in the inner world
    and its effects there can be
    as definite;

and that it does not partake of reality
does not diminish it.
The mountain brook is not shamed
that it does not have the power of the vast ocean;
for it to be a brook
and fulfill a brook's destiny
is the full measure of value that can be given.
The actions we practice on the external world,
the world of stone or wood or flower,
matter little.
These actions may be illusion
and they may not—
but even the reality of their effects
will fade away with the passage of time.
The actions we practice on each other
are of a different order altogether;
for though we may never know that we have
changed reality,
we can alter another's view of it—
for better or for worse.
In either case,
in altering an individual's view
we have altered the individual
and to the degree that they are
changed by that contact
we are responsible for them.
Not to accept this responsibility
is to be more a thief of life
than is a murderer.

—lin ho: *Visions On a Mud Ball*
translated by Chester Valentine

XV

ching: the well

Overland; darkness.
it's the only way to travel
Fragments, stretches, of Interstate 80; from sand and patchy scrub he had moved onto it, seventy-five miles/ an hour ago, and in that time/space had seen nothing, no movement on the highway from horizon to horizon.

Not that Ben had expected to encounter anyone else; whole sections of this route had been blasted away. Unless CenterForce had brought out their road crews, there wasn't much left of 80 between Reno and Sacramento, or from Salt Lake City to the Utah border.

Now he traveled west, toward the darker of the two horizons the Interstate offered. Toward Reno; toward old friends and probably a few enemies; toward sanctuary from CenterForce.

Ahead of him moved an oval of light thrown from his latticed spotbeam. This far out and away from the traveled lanes, a light could be risked; there was, of course, no taillight—it had been the first thing he had removed when he began the conversion of the factory-model cycle.

He thought about it now:

In a crate; packed there a dozen years before, left in a warehouse, moved about through six or seven changes of ownership, and never seen. Never, until Bobby had won it in a poker game; and had died of a shotgun blast on Christopher Street; and had left it to him in his will.

Bobby's mother: *my god, my god, what kind of a world is this, where nineteen-year-old boys leave wills?*

In a crate: the police had tried to impound it, but Ben had thought about it. He had brought the gas and oil with him to the warehouse and gone in through the roof, and Big Tex had set the charges on the main door, and the first and last that the watchman knew of it was when the door came off in a whipcrack explosion and five seconds later a motorcycle shot by him and disappeared into the darkness of West Street.

In this darkness, now, Ben smiled; it was the smile of a father recalling his child's first steps.

Eight hundred miles above him, in plunge it hovered, glistening. At its widest, it was eighteen feet; but half of that was accounted for by the solarcell banks which had the curious appearance of wings—here, where there was no air for wings to beat.

Within the central sphere, an onboard computer noted an anomaly; this first interrupt was quickly followed by a second. A deliberation counted in nanoseconds determined that an unaccounted-for emission of both heat and light was occurring in the sector scanned by this satellite. After beaming down a recognition signal—the computer's analog of a diffident cough—the satellite passed on the information to Houston Satellite Control, which in turn routed it to CenterForce HQ in St. Louis.

Eventually—which is to say, one-fifteenth of a second after the satellite's scanner had first picked it up—the radiation anomaly which was Ben Reed's motorcycle appeared as a moving dot of light on the SouthWestern II Board in CenterForce Operations Control.

Lieutenant Beale noticed it, and grimaced. If it had been a red dot, which would signify up to two dozen or so cyclists; or a green one, indicating from twenty-five to a hundred; or the very rare flash of blue, for runs anything larger than that—if it had been any of these, the interruption of his reading (*Whip Her Snapper*, NighTower Books: Van Nuys, 1973) he might have accepted with good grace, even *esprit de corps*. But this?

Might as well get it over with.

Scratching a cheek that should have been shaved several hours earlier, Beale swiveled to the ComConsole and studded in the Ops Officer. Miss Tomlinson came on; *my luck*, he informed an unspecified god reproachfully, and was confirmed in his dark thoughts by her first comment.

"Heavens!" she scowled at him in three dimensions and living color, "you do look a fright. Have you been sleeping at your desk?"

"No," he said sourly, though he would hardly have admitted it if it were true. "Besides, my appearance doesn't matter, since this is not a social call. I've got a White on the ess-doubleyou-two, and nothing else showing. Patch me in to MacDonald so I can find out what to do about him/her/it."

Tomlinson looked a bit flustered, and it was an interesting intellectual exercise for him to speculate about her hesitation. He thought: *do look a fright? Where does she get those usages, what kind of books does she read?* And the explanation of her odd pause came on like a computer display; confirmation with her words.

"*Captain* MacDonald," she stressed the rank to point up Beale's omission of it, "is currently off call for anything less than a Condition Green. If I could—"

"No, I'll take care of it myself. Tell the Captain hello for me when he checks in and say that I hoped she was nice." Beale studded out, a pleased smile on his face, before Tomlinson could reply.

The white dot had changed position slightly; with an appreciative raise of one eyebrow Beale tapped an ADDITIONAL into the CRT keyboard. Almost instantly the small screen above the keyboard came to life, letters and numbers appearing, altering, stabilizing.

+ + + + +

SPEED:

76.3 mph

ESTIMATED WEIGHT—VEHICLE:

500 lbs

ESTIMATED WEIGHT—OCCUPANT:

175 lbs

ESTIMATED NUMBER IN VEHICLE:

1

ROUTE OR COORDINATE PROGRESSION:

west on nonop/Intst 80

ESTIMATED   PRIMARY   DESTINATION:

reno nevada*****proscribed

ESTIMATED SECONDARY DESTINATION:

carson city nevada*****proscribed

CONFIRMED VEHICLE TYPE:

motorcycle

ESTIMATED   VEHICLE   SPECIFICATIONS:

four stroke
four gear
driveshaft

ESTIMATED VEHICLE IDENTIFICATION:

bmw r 60/modified

ESTIMATED OCCUPANT IDENTIFICATION:

rick moore/fugitive/nam 6382
ed peson/fugitive/wam4219
ben reed/fugitive/wam1554
al jehad/fugitive/wam9935

+ + + + +

All on the fugitive list; weren't there any good citizens anymore, tooling about on cycles?

No, thought Beale, probably not. To most respectable people, the motorcycle was a symbol of anarchy, of violence, of *them*—and you didn't want anyone to think that you had anything in common with *them*. *They* didn't respect the President, or even CenterForce, and they were after your daughters, and if we'd stamped them out when we had the chance . . .

Beale gazed at the CRT display unseeingly. He had

been a motorcycle cop in the old days, before the beginning of the Trouble, first in California and then, when Anna's lungs went bad, in Nevada. A good one, too, before even the clear desert air became too heavy for Anna and he lost her—and then, perhaps because he was thinking about her, lost his right leg as well.

He had wanted to stay on the road; he had shown them that he could ride his old ElectraGlide just as well, and when they wouldn't buy that, he had tried for the new Patrol Bus Corps—though of course it wasn't the same as really being out there, only you and the cycle and the road.

But they wouldn't even accept him for that; then, when the Executive order for the consolidation of the FBI, all police forces, and highway patrols into one agency had come down, and he had been offered the St. Louis job, Beale had thought, *why not?*, and had left behind him his wife and leg and the magic of open land and two wheels.

Out there, now:

a fugitive, yes; heading toward what was left of Reno, a town on the proscribed list, yes; a criminal undoubtedly, and out that far probably a murderer, of CenterForce personnel among others—you couldn't travel far in that territory on a cycle without killing or being killed.

Beale's right hand moved from the CRT keyboard to the Solitaire Target Arming Switch. His fingers flipped back the protective cover and operated the switch. Above it, a white light began to pulse.

Six hundred and twenty-five miles above Nevada, and two hundred miles north of the surveillance satellite, another and much larger object hung in relative motionlessness, securely seated in synchronous majesty. At its earthside point, a six-inch square suddenly appeared, gradually turning black as the small hatch withdrew and pivoted aside. Within, the rounded composition nose of the tiny missile glinted slightly, reflecting the star field; the earth below it was dark.

The missile was a hybrid descendant of the giant ICBM and the RedEye air-to-air rocket; it had the sophisticated guidance system of the former and the heat-seeking capabilities of the latter. Even now the satellite's onboard computer had fed into the missile guidance system the data relayed by Solitaire Control from the surveillance satellite; it gave the target location to within a hundred-square-yard area, and this was more than sufficient for the infrared sensing of the Final Approach subsystem. Like a cyclopean eagle, eye of fire and tail of flame, it would swoop down on a prey that could more easily escape the wrath of the gods.

Beale's right hand moved two inches, to another protective cover; on it, in red letters, were the words *Solitaire Firing One*. The forefinger began to tap without rhythm on the metal cover plate.

Beale had the authority, there was no question of that; it was well within the sphere of action for any of the eight Acting Board Officers to initiate Terminating Measures for Conditions White or Red. Beyond that, there was a possibility of policy complications and such decisions had to be referred to higher authority.

The forefinger tapped.

It had not been Lieutenant Beale then; just Patrolman Beale, and he had only seemed to deal with two kinds of people—those with the steaming radiators, who would either wait for the sun to go down or ask him to call a garage, and those who wanted to open her up and see what she could do. Ofttimes, if Beale's ominous presence hadn't slowed them down, she showed what she could do; she could spread her passengers and herself over two hundred yards of highway. He had never been able to get used to those sights, though he might see them every day for weeks on end.

The forefinger tapped.

But during the winter months, when few drivers took the northern cross-country route, and particularly during the graveyard shift—then, it was magic. The roar of the twelve hundred cc's of the Harley engine, and the unearthly silence when he would draw onto the shoulder and stop for a cigarette. The stars, so many stars, and the open land and the road, and all of it was his, if only for that moment.

He missed it; it was a pain and a longing. Was it because then he had been with Anna, was that it? Partly; but in his memory of the night land he had traveled, it was the stars he missed most keenly. Here in St. Louis, on a clear night, one might see the Big Dipper, or the constellation of Orion, or Polaris; but in the Nevada night, standing on a rise above the Interstate, the stars seemed almost to surround you—and it seemed so easy to believe that this great ball on which you stood was part of the universal magic in someone else's sky.

A change in the CRT display caught Beale's eye, but it was a moment before he could tell which line had changed.

+ + + + +

SPEED: 0 mph/vehicle stationary/systems not operating

+ + + + +

Didn't mean anything, of course; the residual heat from the engine would be quite suffcient for a system that could home in on a lighted cigarette—and which once had during a trial demonstration, creating a momentary gap in the CenterForce Command Staff.

Beale looked up at the SW II Board; there was a white ring around the now-motionless white dot, confirming the CRT display. He, whoever he was (or she, if the computer's information was incomplete), was parked on Interstate 80, just over a hundred miles outside Reno.

The forefinger tapped: more slowly.

He was sitting out there, in the night.

Beale frowned at the Board, and studded in the full map overlay. Mm-hmm. There he was, not too far down from Winnemucca; what was the name of that bar in Winnemucca, where Beale had stopped every time through? He could remember *her* name: Kathleen, and she had been as Irish and as beautiful as the name. She had brought him the beer, and he had told her about Anna and what was going to happen, and the sort of person he would have to be—and Kathleen had understood, and there had been talk and even laughter from time to time.

Then Anna had gone into the hospital again, and he sat by her bed for nineteen hours while the respirator lost its battle with nature. And when he had come back to the trailercamp that had been home, eyes unblinking and stony that the inevitable had actually happened, Kathleen had been there waiting.

The forefinger, against the metal coverplate: motionless.

The days of his leave had passed, too quickly; his holding her in his arms, at first in the vertiginous fear of bereavement, had begun the whisperings of a magic that was reflected in her eyes.

Back on the ElectraGlide, on duty; reality returning in slices, and Kathleen always there to remind him that there was a future as well as a past.

Then the culvert bridge, and the joyriding youngsters in the truck spooked into headlong flight; the fishtailing vehicle's gongsmack, and the stone abutment. If he had not been in radio contact with HQ only seconds before, he might have bled to death; as it was, he had been in surgery for nineteen hours—exactly as long as it had taken Anna to die.

Kathleen had tried to see him in the hospital, but he would not permit it; he had sent her a note, terse and cold, asking her to go back to Winnemucca until he could figure out what was happening in his life. She had sent him an answering note, refusing to leave, but when they brought him home to the trailer there was no sign of her.

He talked to her once on the phone—she had gone back to Winnemucca, to the bar—and had tried to explain that he was not what he had been before; that he couldn't hold her to something she had not bargained for. Kathleen had said that he was making a mistake, but that when the day came that he wanted to correct it she would be waiting.

Beale's hand traversed the two inches back to the Solitaire Target Arming Switch: his fingernail flicked against the now-upright coverplate.

The St. Louis assignment had come, and he had made the move, and he had thought; then he had written to her, and the letter had come back *Addressee Unknown*. A friend in the Sector had checked, a few weeks later, and found both the bar and the furnished rooms above it to be deserted.

He was out there, in the night; as Beale had been, when Anna had been in the world, when the touch of Kathleen's hand on his shoulder had meant the world would still be there.

Out there, hey: what are you seeing? Are you seeing that you're surrounded by stars you can almost touch? Are you seeing those stars and planets and knowing that you're a part of that universe? Are you seeing, in the spaces between the stars, someone you left behind, someone who could have made it all matter?

Beale's hand turned the Solitaire Target Arming Switch to the OFF position; the white light above the switch ceased its pulsing, and far above and to the west, a six-inch square of metal pivoted and moved outward to its previous position.

Out there, in the night:

Ben took a last drag from the joint and, holding it, looked up at the million-lighted celestial hemisphere. Unbidden, Amy back in Denver his thought: *Amy would like this.*

Amy: what is she doing now?

And why do I care?

XVI

ku: work on what has been spoiled

SARA'S DAREDEVIL CLOWN

Everybody says that I'm a maniac for thinking
    I could get from you the right time of day
Everybody says I'm like a ship that is sinking
    while for you it's strictly anchors aweigh
Everybody says that you're a minefield in the country
    and just hoping that I'll walk over you
Everybody says that you're some no-fault insurance
    with the premiums a year overdue
    *

    But babe, you got me doing dances
    and you got me taking chances
    and just acting like a daredevil clown
    I just hope you realize
    in that world behind your eyes
    that for me it's still a long way down
    *

Went up to my shrink today and told him of my lady gay
    and watched him curling up in a ball
He said I didn't have to pay, it didn't matter anyway,
    might see me again in the Fall
Wrote my mother home a letter, told her things were
    getting better,
    gave her all the details on you
Now there's no one at her phone, my letters come back
    marked Unknown,
    my postcards come back marked Untrue
    *

And babe, you got me doing dances . . .
    *

Everybody says that I'm a masochist for waiting
    just to find out what game you're gonna play
Everybody says the little world that you're creating's
    gonna blow up on the very next day
Everybody says that they know easy ways of suicide
    if I'm about to rip up my brain
Everybody says that if I'm gonna take that final ride
    I oughta do it minus the pain
    *

Now babe, you got me doing dances . . .
    *

                              —from a rock song, circa 1977

XVII

shih: the army

(EXTRACT FROM CORRO MANUSCRIPTS/FRAG. 88d)
. . . in St. Louis, Missouri. Immediately following the assassination of the Acting Director, however, it was conceded that proper control and security could no longer be maintained in the setting which had been the Bureau's since its very inception. Accordingly, the Consolidation Bill was signed into law by the President, and immediately thereafter began the transferral of information from the Bureau's Washington files to the new CenterForce databanks.

It was determined that physically transferring the records was too hazardous an undertaking; therefore, transfer was accomplished by computers over land lines. The amount of information to be transferred was so vast that, not counting delays occasioned by sabotage to phone lines, it was nearly a year before the task was completed.

Software specialists then were assigned to program this information into a vast cross-correlative network that would mesh with the data produced by Center-Force's extensive information-gathering network.

This project was fourteen months in process, and during this time there was a diffuse public feeling of uncertainty regarding the CenterForce computer. Radical left and underground sources nicknamed the computer "Big Brother" and claimed it would end personal freedom in the United States; others, more moderate, were concerned about the possibility of computer error, particularly in the projected operation by the Center-

Force computer of what were to be called Robuses; each Robus was to be controlled by the computer without human intervention or intermediaries, and it was planned that eventually these remotely operated vehicles, with their highly sophisticated sensor and weapons systems, would replace the manned Patrol buses.

That this Robus program was not, in fact, activated probably was not due to public opinion, which was having a negligible effect on Administration policy at this time, but rather to certain technical difficulties which could not be overcome to the satisfaction of the engineers on the project.

The emergence of CenterForce as the law of the land produced, not too surprisingly, several major conflicts in certain urban and rural areas. Reports of these conflicts, spread by illegal radio and TV stations, often with film records that had been smuggled out of the areas, led for a time to further public unrest; a massive public relations campaign by CenterForce officials, highlighted by their own filmed records of the conflicts, was eventually successful in turning public opinion into a wholehearted support of CenterForce and its work.

The Proscription Act, which was activated after certain cities withheld cooperation from CenterForce—San Francisco, California; Reno, Nevada; Atlanta, Georgia; and New Orleans, Louisiana, among them (New York City, in spite of the popular sentiment, did not openly oppose CenterForce; however, the agency found its task quite as difficult, if not more, as had its predecessor)—was criticized even by some members of the Administration as being a divisive and polarizing influence. It cannot be denied, however, that this admittedly extreme action did have the effect of greatly reducing the CenterForce workload and casualty rate.

The Act did, of course, create certain hardships for those . . .

XVIII

hsu: waiting

"And none of you did anything? You were all just going to stand there and let it happen?"

They were all in a circle, hand clasping hand, in Bigdome; all except Marc, who looked at them in puzzled angry concern, and asked the question.

"But Marc, there were a dozen of them!"

"And there are nearly a hundred of us."

Another voice: "They had knives. I think one or two of them had guns."

"And would they have killed you all, just so Sonny could get to Jill? Are we another Jewish ghetto, where two storm troopers rounded up six hundred Jews for the gas chambers?"

For a long moment Marc tried to keep the hard expression locked in; but it wouldn't hold, and perhaps that was better, for it would do no good to become Stern Daddy here where every person must learn to be Daddy and Mommy to everyone else.

"People, now: listen. The whole point of what we're doing here is to avoid the violence trip, but that isn't just for us. If it's only for us it *has* no point. Like in karate the ethic is 'I have superior power, but, having it, I will not hurt you, as I will not let you hurt me.' Now that's alright, but Aikido goes it one better. 'As I do not wish for you to harm me, I also do not wish for you to harm yourself, either in body or in spirit. Therefore it is not enough simply to defend myself; I must prevent you from making the attack.'

"It's the same old thing—*satyagraha*, truth force. What we have to do . . ."

The circle, she thought: StarChild, enclosing Marc, a protective magic—and she was outside it.

Jill stood on the rise north of the cluster of domes and other structures. It was twilight, quiet and still. Across the sunred flatland the air lay heavy; in the distance rose a sandstone butte, a dryfall of dustblown sand now coursing down its sides.

She could hear every word of Marc's, and most of the responses; it sounded strange, as though they were talking about someone else. Marc had wanted her to be there, but the very thought of it had dragged at her, sucked at her energy, and she had done a traumatized-girl scene that Marc, surprisingly, had believed, and he had said no more about it.

But her body was not her own now.

In the center of her being: a lock of sea-rough metal, never seen by land-eyes, never known by those she knew. The ferric strangeness fed out along her veins, limbs, senses; as now she was outside the circle by choice, so since the death-grinned alienness of the threat had she been outside what any of the others at StarChild could know. She did not know what they could have done; she only knew that none of them had done it. *If someone came into our house and tried to hit Mom, Daddy wouldn't let him.*

Family, Marc had said: we are a web of love that is a family.

But it wasn't real, not real in the way she had always known. The family can't be invaded; it isn't separate people who can be isolated.

Her own family had not been love, the kind of love she needed and had found here—but this family was not the wall around her world that she had known before, the wall that let in friendship and new adventure but kept out darkness and the unknown hungers.

Her body was not her own now.

Beneath her unsandalled foot, a rock, dull-pointed. Jill pressed her sole down against it. Harder.

Harder.

When the tears came, it was not enough release. Still the lock lay within her, a weighted and waiting small strangeness. Sonny had died before he could touch her; but he had impregnated her with the sperm of mindless fear, and now within her gestated something she could not understand.

And the lock within her sang. *You are not yours, you are mine. As I am within you, so are you within me, never to be free to touch the living world again until the Key finds me. Now your life must be a waiting for that Key, and your only article of faith: that it exists,*
out there, in the darkness.

XIX

k'an: the abysmal

Marble Fork
(date deleted)

Hiya Charlie,

I don't really know why I'm writing this, but I guess
it's to get rid of some of the crap in my head. Used to be
able to talk to Martha (some, anyway), but since she's
gone it's been like solitary.

Yeah, really *is* solitary now. This one you won't believe. (I mean, you'll believe it happened but you won't
believe I could let it happen.) That crazy daughter of
mine's gone out to live at that hippie place outside of
town. I tried to get some sense into her, but Marriette
takes after her grandma on the other side, and she just
went and there wasn't a hell of a lot I could do. I mean
for one thing I'm not an officer anymore, and I damn
sure can't go over to that bastard Grogan (told you
about him a couple of letters ago) and ask him to do
anything about it. And even if she is underage I'd look
like a fucking idiot going out there and trying to drag
her back.

But those kids all look kind of scrawny and under-
nourished, let alone dirty, and she'll probably get enough
of that crap in a couple of weeks and come back with
her tail between her legs. I just hope she doesn't catch
anything while she's there.

Some kid was through town and needed some money
and sold me one of those Armalite AR-7s for $15, can
you believe! I didn't even know any of those were still
around. If you're interested make me an offer, because
with the 15 and the 16 and that Stoner setup I've got
I don't really need it. The kid had been firing the thing

from the smell and when I asked he just said target practice. Sure, he's strapped for cash and he's going to waste rounds on practice. Probably some cop somewhere with a slug from this baby in him.

But you know, that shows you how dumb these kids are, why Center will eventually get them all. That kid wasn't heeled with anything else, and now he's out there with whatever amount of gas he could buy, and *you know* without a weapon he's just not going to last long.

Couple of funny things happening around here, aside from my idiot kid.

I don't know how true it is, but I heard that a bunch of Grogan's punks went out to the hippie place and started hassling them. Seems Grogan shows up then, drops one of his own and does a pretty-as-you-please apology, and splits. He's had the rest of the bunch that went out on work details around town, and that I know because I've seen it. Those nuts are unpredictable, though, and one of them might decide to return the compliment Grogan gave that guy. I'm not really worried that any of those punks would have gone near Marriette. They know who she is and they aren't that *dumb*.

The other thing, and this should really give you a laugh, is that I think we've got us a Federal around here. I could be wrong, but I carried the tin around here for a long time and we were always getting those wiseasses in and out when the hard silo sites down south were still manned. So I really think I can spot them, and this guy has got the smell.

They call him Chino or China, doesn't matter which, maybe because of this Fu Manchu mustache he's got or because he's all the time mouthing off with this oriental wisdom Buddhist crap. I think he's got that going with some little story about spending time in Japan, to explain why he's so good at the rough stuff. Most of these punks are pretty good street fighters, though I could probably take them, but this Chino's just too good. Three of them jumped him in my bar the

other night and he gave them a pair of punches apiece
and that's all, brother. I think he got the first one without even spilling his drink. Chino has all the moves and
he didn't pick them up in an alley. And that's another
thing. Anybody else could handle himself like that
would really be pushing things, but Chino just kind of
follows everybody around and doesn't start anything.
Sits and watches, the kind of way you or I can spot but
doesn't mean anything to anyone else. I guess the only
reason Grogan hasn't made him his lieutenant or something is that he can't figure him out.

So, like I say, I could be wrong, but I don't think so.
I'll nose around a little bit and see if I can really pin
him, because it might come in handy to have something
to use for juice around here someday.

So how are things up in Nebraska? Got a letter from
Davis in Aspen and he said you told him you might
go in as Supervisor in the Arms Maintenance Bus Shed
in Omaha. From what I hear, you'd have to move into
the city or buy a tank, because every nut with the price
of a mortar is trying to take out a bus up there. Even
flying in they lost a couple. Really bad.

You never did tell me what you want for that P-38.
You really ought to sell it to me, I've got the brass for
it because I have one of the postwar models but I don't
fire it much. The damn thing is just too light with that
alloy crap, and I'm always wondering if it's going to
blow up in my face. I've still got that accurized .45, but
I'd rather just leave it in the bar and have the Walther
to carry around with me.

I don't know what I'm going to do about Marriette
if she doesn't come back in a while. Could just leave her
out there, I don't know, but I almost think I'd rather
have her messing around with these bike punks than
out there. These guys only want one thing, but those
people could start making her think all sorts of funny
things and I don't know what the hell would finally
happen to her. Maybe if I can get a line on this Chino
guy I can get him to do something about it.

The only reason I even bother about it, I guess, is that I keep thinking, what would Martha think? Dumb, huh?

There's a courier going down to the Flagstaff Mail Center today, so I better close this up so I can make sure it gets out today.

> Yr ole buddy,
> EDDY

P.S. Don't forget to let me know what you want to do on that P-38, and if you're interested in the Armalite.

> EG

XX

kuan: contemplation

Senator North stood for a long time at his office window, watching the gulls gliding along the East River, far below. He was trying to put off making an unpleasant decision.

No; that was not quite true. He had, he realized, already made the decision. What he was trying to do now was pretend that time was not moving, that in a few minutes he would not be standing on the dais in the great Meeting Room making the speech that could cost him his career.

Ted North was a man with principles which had outlived their usefulness, at least for anyone who aspired to a long political career. He still believed in the American Dream, and in the documents and principles that had inspired that dream, even now—when even the most naive and optimistic conceded that the dream had become a nightmare. North, too, thought it a nightmare; the difference between him and his companions was that he still thought the United States could awaken from the horribly real fantasy into which it had descended.

Senator Theodore North's office was on the twenty-seventh floor of what had the official title of, simply, The Government Building; unofficially it was called The Headstone. Some years before it had been the U.N. Office Building; but that organization had conveniently voted to relocate on Sardinia, less than two years before the destruction of most government structures in Washington had forced its own relocation—New York being the logical choice, to the chagrin of many.

A few hundred yards west of The Headstone was a small mall bordered with dying shrubbery. At the mall's northern end was a curving stairway which led, in one of those geographical quirks, to the foot of Forty-third Street; along the wall that bordered this stairway was a quote from the Bible which touched on swords and plowshares.

Parked on Forty-third, near the railing leading to the mall, was a battered and begrimed station wagon. Behind the blanket-covered front seat, the rest of the automobile seemed packed from floor to ceiling with an assortment of cardboard boxes and small packing cases. In spite of the fact that the vehicle, a very disreputable '73 model, had been parked on this spot for seven hours, no policeman had disturbed it, even ticketed it. There *was* an out-of-order note on the parking meter, which examination would have proved true; there *was* a small metal fixture above the license plate which read CLERGY.

Yet even if anyone had taken especial note of the car, it is doubtful that they would have noticed that one of the windows on the side nearest the stairs was opened an inch; it is even more doubtful that they would have observed the minute vibration of the car from time to time, as though somehow weight were being shifted around inside it.

The phone buzzed. North ignored it for a moment, looking down at the discolored water; then, with an interior rueful smile, pressed his lips together and let time start running again.

"North."

"Ted? Glad I caught you." It was Jerry Socol, North's PR man/confidant/friday/demon. Jerry was immensely likable, which was a commercial asset; after a fashion, and in his own way, very aware of moral issues and ethical implications, which was not particularly com-

mercial but which he kept under control. Jerry honestly
wanted the best of everything for his boss, and this
translated as The Presidency. North could save the
country, Jerry was sure of it; and that justified a lot.
With this total belief, Jerry could have hands and heads
stepped on when it appeared necessary, and if he had
been asked about some of these acts/events/unfor-
tunate occurrences while being monitored by a pneu-
mograph, a sphygmomanometer, and a Wheatstone
bridge—the instruments would show no change, no
change at all.

"Don't be too glad," said the Senator. "I've decided
to go ahead with it."

There was a long pause at the other end of the line.
Then, "Ted, I don't know what to say. Nothing I
haven't said a dozen times already. You're the boss,
you want to go out on the floor in front of people some
of who are still your friends, and open a vein, I can't
stop you. You're entitled. It just seems so damn silly
to do it for nothing, to waste it. I think your career is
worth more than that."

"Or your career?"

"You didn't say that, did you?"

North sighed. "No. I didn't. And we *have* been all
over this before, Jer. First, I'm not positive I'm going to
get shot down over there, and second, even if I am I
think it's worth it to get things started. We can't go on
the way we're going. *Somebody* has to introduce the
Amnesty Bill, sooner, or there won't *be* any later. Christ,
hasn't anyone even heard of the Civil War?"

"The *first* Civil War," Jerry amended. "And what do
you think would have happened to anyone then who
suggested that the Blues and the Grays just throw down
their guns and let bygones be bygones?"

Senator North was beginning to feel an odd mental
lethargy. "Well, nobody tried, so we don't know, do we?
At least this time we'll know. See you after the speech."
He disconnected before Jerry could reply.

In the elevator, the moving light a countdown: *23, 22, 21, 20, 19.*

Maybe Jerry was right; maybe it *was* a foolish gesture. *16, 15, 14.*

Or worse? Was it just a grandstand play for him? *11, 10, 9.*

Perhaps for an ego game in his head? The noble statesman, sacrificed fighting The Good Fight? *6, 5, 4.*

No. No; he had examined these doubts before, and discarded them. There was a point to what he was about to do; there was a purpose. *1.*

With a hydraulic sigh the doors parted. Senator Theodore North stepped out and glanced at his watch. Yes; there was enough time. He headed out through the glassed double doorway and moved along the curving pavement toward the squat modern architecture of what was now called (in the same tone of simplicity as its companion) the Meeting Hall.

The two girls, walking in the opposite direction, were six feet away from him when it happened. Many times, in the subsequent course of their lives, Merilee and Jo wondered what might have happened to them had Jo not spotted a run in Merilee's nylon, causing them to stop for two seconds outside the Meeting Hall doors, thus putting them a safe distance away from the Senator when his body exploded.

It only seemed to explode, of course; subsequent examination indicated that three projectiles had entered the body. One shattered the pelvic area and destroyed essential organs; another, entering the upper left side without striking the left arm, destroyed the heart and both lungs; the last entered the head under and slightly to the rear of the left ear, causing instantaneous destruction of the brain from hydrostatic shock.

Intensive analysis of trajectories tended toward a theory of one sharpshooter only, firing a burst of three rounds; that all three were so well placed was ascribed to a combination of skill and luck on the part of the unknown assailant.

On the evening of that same day, firemen answering a call on Broome Street in downtown Manhattan arrived to find an old station wagon aflame. The gasoline tank had ruptured and the heat was intense; the vehicle was totally destroyed before the fire could be put out.

A laboratory analysis of the ashes might have indicated the presence of human remains, but such a test was not made.

XXI

chin: progress

Three memories of Reno.

Memory One:

He had been (five? six?) just a little boy; the train was called *The City Of San Francisco*, and they had got on in Chicago. From the window, at night, Reno; out there in the middle of nowhere, this thing that looked like just one brightly lit street, as though some giant had been building a town elsewhere and had mislaid this one piece of it. Or maybe it was one of those fake towns they made movies in; he had seen pictures of one in his Book of Knowledge.

Memory Two:

He was fourteen, and his mother had given up. She was waiting out the time for the divorce, and for some reason had taken him out of school and brought him along. For the first week or so she had acted strange, and wouldn't let Ben out of her sight, but then she had seemed to relax.

The girl was a dancer at the Golden Dollar; he saw her in the show toward the end of the second week, and nearly every show she did after that for ten days until she noticed him. She was twenty-two, her name was Glenda, and she lived in a little trailer in a trailer park about six blocks from the club. When he walked her home, they sat on the little couch and talked for a while and then she asked where his mother was staying and went into the bedroom and talked on the phone.

She called to him and he came in and she was in

the bed with the blanket up to her hips; she had worn
less than this in the show, but it was not at all the same.
When his clothes were off and he was on the bed beside
her, she had kissed him and moved her head down his
body and he had exploded right then; but she had smiled
and not minded and had made it happen again and
again through the night, with her body and her hands
and her lips.

For three weeks, every moment she was not working
or sleeping, they were together. Then she had to go to
Los Angeles for a show, and Ben and his mother had
to leave before she returned.

Glenda had said once, during those three weeks, that
he would hurt people someday. He had not understood,
and she had said to forget it, and he had; but he had
not forgotten her.

Memory Three:

Just a little more than a year ago, now; CenterForce
had still been hot and heavy about the Proscribed
towns, and it had been bloody hell getting here. Not
tootling along 80 like a king, that was for damn sure;
but would you believe trying to come up three-nine-five
from Berdoo? He probably hadn't spent fifty miles of
it on the road, what with both CenterFuzz and the
target-practice nuts who thought he was fair game—as,
of course, he legally was.

But he had made it, never really doubting that he
would; and there wasn't very much left of the town he
had remembered. Lot of the buildings burnt down or
blasted—the only thing that *could* get through the
rubble now was a cycle—and when he'd gone to look
for it, gone too; where the trailerpark had been was a
refuse dump.

Ben found most of them at the Silver Barfly; Big Tex,
Sparky, Grogan and Trina, and the rest. Everyone getting wasted on righteous dope and tequila, and for once
not worrying about CenterFuzz, unless they decided to
drop the Bomb. This, of course, always became the big
number during the paranoia downside of tripping; you

could figure about how long ago somebody'd got off on something by how often looked up—knowing full well that if the Bomb *did* come they wouldn't have any warning but the flash, and probably think *it* was a delayed rush from whatever dope they were doing.

It had been kind of nice, kind of weird; no really big hassles, though Trina could certainly have set one up between Ben and Grogan if she had wanted to.

Three memories: all feeding to the fourth, to now.

But, now, another memory:
Amy: what is she doing now?
And why do I care?
Probably getting stoned. Probably getting royally balled in that weird little back room. She sure as hell probably never hurts for that. Dynamite fucking chick. Wonder why she dug to do a number with me?

Ben could not imagine why this thought came, at this moment. After Glenda it had always been there; *of course* they had always wanted to ball him. Even the ones who said they didn't, and cried; they'd cry, but they'd fuck. So, what about Amy, why shouldn't she . . . ?

For a long time, through the suicide hours, Ben sat beside the cycle, mind roving and prodding and poking, occasionally coming back to Amy and caroming away again. Amy seemed somehow linked with Glenda, and coming back to Reno was doing a number in his head with that fact, and did he, no he didn't, not really *want* to know.

Not yet; not just yet.

XXII

li: the clinging

BLOODBIRD

1.
he is there
waiting
following the many-speckled track
the droplets
ovals, crowned; leaning in the direction of her flight
the red crowns (on linoleum, on wood) of
    dark, coursing, pumping reality/royalty
                          and being

2.
he has been there for a long time
                but for a time
    his gaze was averted; her darknesses
                            unperceived
and her movements toward hollow coronation
                                unknown

3.
he is there
        still
and now the wounds attract
                    his porcelain gaze
a wing, here, a flutter
    there a talon flexed
                    on the dead branch of his fears
now, again, a movement below
spatter

        and he takes wing
hovering, for a time, on the currents of sorrow
                                descending, then,
with outstretched talons
4.
princess, lover, victim, blood
                                he descends
talons search out her wounds
                                unerringly
with the terrible finality of his grip
        the wounds cease to flow
and in her last measureless instant
                                she thinks she has been saved

                        —from *The Lethargy Of Dragons*
                        by Perdurabo,
                        Phoenix Free Press of Los Angeles
                        (date deleted)

XXIII
heng: duration

. . . I often wonder what it was that brought me here in the first place and, more importantly, what keeps me here. I suppose I could tell myself it is inertia, but more likely it is a combination of fear and an old man's reluctance to pull up roots.

Even were I to depart from Marble Fork, where would I go? Those city hospitals would laugh in my face, those that still remember what a general practitioner *is*. And even if they did hire me, I should imagine I would still feel as dispensable as one of those throwaway plastic thermometers they use these days.

Here, at least the people of the commune need me. Curing hepatitis is perhaps an unromantic way to pass the time, but it is still preferable to initialing forms in some vast concrete structure in one of those dying cities.

It all seems to hang in such precarious balance, however. I have mentioned here before my fears that soon everything we know will collapse like a house of cards. Thus far, I have been wrong, but soon it must happen. I am reminded of the example of the teacup whose molecules move in random motion; if they should all move in the same direction at once, the teacup will dash itself to pieces. In physics the odds against this happening are incalculable—but what of society? How much random violent movement of its particles can it sustain, particularly when more and more such particles begin to move along the same violent path? When will the world we know dash itself to pieces on the rocks of hatred?

—from the daily journal of
Dr. M. J. Michelson
(all dates deleted)

XXIV

lu: treading

I was on a very paranoid trip, and it didn't help any
to realize it as it was happening. Ancient gag line, now
gagging up in the synapses as we moved through the
giant toilet: *paranoids have as much right to be followed as anyone else.* No consolation, not at all. I
mean, is it possible to have delusions of persecution
while you're *being* persecuted? I don't know.

It was a toilet, or very like one. Big long hallways,
porcelain or a linoleum plastic that looked a lot like it;
plumbing, and I was the piece of shit that was being
flushed down it. I searched for things to shore up the
analog. Um. Lights? No lights in toilets, not *inside* the
things. The attendants? Um. No; you don't have honor
guards when you shit, one on each side like I had now,
unless your parents were really into toilet training and
fascism at the same time.

Holy shit.

Not a religious experience, no, but the analog had
suddenly turned on me viciously. The guards that were
tootling me along: wearing *paper* uniforms. It made
sense—disposable, I suppose they have a few from time
to time that freak and vomit all over the place. But
still . . .

. . . besides this, I had other subplots going. Why was
I here? Was it Amy turned me in? Or Frank? Or—what
was his name, the bike freak she balled? Nobody knew
that cat, he could have been heat. Wow, zingo. Two
buses beside me and the hypump with ThoraQuel, which
is, ah yes, fighting a losing battle with the acid. Of

course they would find out and eventually dose me with niacin or something so I could be sane by their standards at least for the interview.

A fluorescent door obligingly disappeared as we went into a room and they sat me down on a chair that had no back but wasn't a stool, and they left me. No chains to the floor, and they were perfectly correct in their actions. Where could I go?

He seemed to appear the same way the door had disappeared, and I began to suspect that I was not paying close enough attention to the world; I would try to do better, but what kept distracting me? And what did I think about when I was distracted?

"I beg your pardon?" I knew he had said something to me, and it seemed wise to indicate that I had noticed even if I couldn't tell him what it was.

"I said, I'm Dr. Lane. And you?"

"I'm not a doctor." It was nothing I could help; let him make of it what he might.

"I didn't imagine you were." Aha; snobbery. "Could you give me your name?"

"Gretsch."

"First name?"

"No. Last."

"No. I mean what is your first name?"

"Oh. Gibson, but everyone calls me Hoot, of course."
Dr. Lane frowned. "Of course?"

I frowned in return, matching him nasolabial fold for nasolabial fold. "You're not a historian." It was an implied rebuke, and he inferred it correctly.

"Well, Mr.—Hoot?" He smiled questioningly; I nodded but kept frowning for a moment. "Address?"

"Yes, but like on the card there that has all the other answers too, No Fixed."

"I see. Why do you suppose you're here, Hoot?"

"Because some people held me and pumped I guess about twenty-five milligrams of ThoraQuel into me and then brought me here."

He wasn't going to be any help. "Why do you suppose they did that?"

I wasn't going to be any help either. "Because they're paid to."

Dr. Lane sighed. "Mr. Gretsch, you're intelligent enough to know what I mean when I ask these questions. Now——"

The ThoraQuel had all but conceded defeat to the acid; it might have handled three to five hundred mikes without any big problem, but I had dropped twelve, bracketed with speed for a protective escort. All the trank was doing now was to coat my body with about an inch of hardening rubbery air that made moving a subject of thought and preparation. My mind, on the other head, was running around the walls and beating on the lighting fixtures and sliding under the glass of a framed picture of Dr. Lane's family and trying to see if it could get away from me and the Doctor by going into the intercom and down through the wire into the wall. I couldn't quite figure out how it might be done; the multiplicity of holes in the speaker made it seem a dangerous proposition.

"—if we're going to accomplish anything you're going to have to cooperate."

"Will I have to have my head shaved?"

"What?"

My, my. He *really* wasn't a historian. I would have to be gentle with him. "I'd really like to help you, Doctor, honestly I would, but I don't know what it is you want me to say."

"Just the truth, Mr. Hoot. That's all."

"Mr. Gretsch or Hoot; no variations, please. Have I lied?"

He sighed again. "No, uh, uh, Hoot. You haven't lied. You haven't really said anything. Would you like to rest for a while and do this later?"

Cooperate. I should cooperate. "Oh. Well, I'm not tired, but if you don't really feel up to it I suppose there's no real rush. Is there a place where I can stay, or would it be better for me to go home?"

I had thought that if I phrased it that way, and he was really tired, he might just say yes and let me go away, but he just smiled tiredly and said, "I think we can make you comfortable here, Hoot. I'll talk to you again in a couple of days."

He went out, and after a while I thought of something to ask him, but the door wouldn't open when I tried it. Neither would anything else; the desk drawers, the vidiphone, the intercom—I had to try them all carefully several times to make sure that it wasn't just the acid and that I hadn't somehow managed to jam/break everything.

Then a guy in one of the paper suits came in; he was big, like Big Tex, and was wearing a Big Tex mask on his face. "Why do you have that on?" I asked.

"To get you out of here," he answered, and it didn't make any sense to me. Why should it matter to me what an attendant looked like?—I'd have to go with him anyway. Maybe they wanted me to feel at home.

"Well, it's very nice of you," I said.

The attendant stopped, looking up and down the toilet-tube hall, and then stared at me closely. "Oh, shit," he said. "What a time for you to be wasted. That's all we fucking need."

I was sorry if I was inconveniencing him, though I couldn't see just how; I tried to apologize, but he just told me to keep quiet. We went through a lot of stair-ways and halls—it was a very complicated toilet—and went by a desk that had a guard stretched out across it sleeping; I didn't see how he could sleep in such an uncomfortable position. Then we went down in an elevator, a big, dirty one that had padding around the sides, I supposed for violent people.

We went out onto a loading dock; it was dark out. There was a truck with lettering on its side that said *SugarKing Bakery, Boulder, Colorado* on the side, and the attendant with the Big Tex mask made me get in the back on a mat and then shut the door.

After the truck had been moving for a while I got curious and rapped on the little window in front until the attendant opened it. "When are you going to take that mask off?" I asked him.

He smiled and said, "Get some sleep. When you wake up you won't see the mask, I promise."

And of course Tex was right.

—excerpt from *Happy Hunting Ground;*
   or, At Play With The Lords Of The Unfelt;
   article in *CRYSTAL*, Aries/Unicorn Summer Edition
   (date deleted), by G. M. "Hoot" Gretsch

XXV

p'i: standstill

The magic word for today
 is progress
 or, as some would say,
 Progress or *Progress* or PROGRESS or
 !PROGRESS!
It is a magic word because,
 like most magic words,
 it can cause change by the simple fact of its
 existence.
Indeed, for many of us
 it is not simply a word of power
 but a power itself—
 a god.
We say:
I will do this
 not for myself or my desires
 but for progress
I must go from this state of being
 to this one over here
 not because I am not content
 but for progress.
We are asked
 perhaps by a man with a lantern
 perhaps by a child—
 what is it,
 this which you call progress?
We make answer and say
 it is a striving

it is an evolving
it is change for the better
but on reflection we find
that of these three answers
the first is observation
·   the second is heart's hope
and the third is an unrealized dream.
And the child asks again:
we make answer and say
one must strive toward a future goal.
And the child asks:
But if the goal is always in the future,
how can it be reached?
And we make answer and say
the purpose of one's life
is in the striving.
Then, says the child,
if the goal matters not,
and attaining the goal matters not,
we strive only to effect change
even when content with things as they are?
And we make no answer.
And the child says:
I worship a great tree
for it gives me shade;
it lets me play in its branches.
I worship our garden
for it gives my mother and father and I
good things to eat;
I worship the eagle and the horse and the fish
for they are free and beautiful.
The child says:
I could not give my life's moments
to a *word*;
I could not worship a *word*.

—lin ho: *Visions On A Mud Ball*
translated by Chester Valentine

XXVI

ts'ui: gathering together

Over the rubble: gear down, nurse her, tease her; watch out for rough-edge metal, broken glass—those tires have been your life in the past, and they might be again before long.

Reno had changed slightly, but only slightly, for the better since the last time Ben had seen it. The main drag was pretty well cleared of rubble and garbage except for a few mounds here and there. The major change was that now at least one of the power stations had to be operating; there were a fair number of lighted buildings along the street, and no sound of generators running on gasoline.

The Silver Barfly. About forty bikes in the lot beside it; there were, of course, no cars, though Ben saw one four-wheeler he recognized—a Land Rover with fore and aft machinegun mounts. Tex would be around somewhere.

Ben locked and chained the BMW; opening the seat, he reached up and threw a small toggle switch, then took from the tool kit an object about the size of a pencil flashlight and stuck it in the breast pocket of his jacket. A friend in Nebraska had set it up for him a few years before; if anyone were to tamper with the bike, the penlight would beep what could well turn out to be an electronic death knell.

In the bar:
hey, baby, what's happening?
oh, wow, hey, it's Ben; where you been, man?
You come from East? What they doing there now?

*Hear about Sparky? Yeah, CenterFuzz snuffed him.
Say what? Yeh, Tex's around someplace; just got in a
couple hours ago on 80, funny you didn't see him.*

Bad beer; Ben nursed a glass for an hour, got told
six or seven times who'd got themselves killed/jailed/
balled/born; he went out and looked at the cycle for a
time, and then walked.

It was still a garbage heap, of course; nothing could
alter the time/space track of his life, make him become
the Ben Reed who would be standing on this spot looking at one specific small trailer among a herd of them,
orangewood light through the small curtained window.
Then: the bed. Now: an engine block, a bent hood,
twisted front forks from a Harley 1200. Then: her voice.
Now: somewhere in the dump, the breeze knocking
metal against metal in oriental rhythm. Then: her eyes.
Now: a few bright stars fading in bloodlight dawn.

Ben was not in love with a memory; he did not yearn
for the past—in fact, rarely thought about it; no desire
to be fourteen again.

But what had happened to her? When it had all come
down, so quickly in one sense and so slowly in another,
how had she opted? Was she in one of the Shitties, one
of the urbs, as the "legal" towns were called? Was she
married, with a couple of kids, to some straight who
bowed and yessirred to CenterFuzz?

Or was she Outside somewhere?

Was she trapped or was she free?

XXVII

sui: following

AGENT: Jonathan Gansell/S14 B2a
LOCATION: Marble Fork, Arizona
DATE: (deleted)
COVER OPERATION/PROCEDURE: (deleted)
REPORT NO.:   45
TEXT: Operational climate at this location remains stable. Terry Grogan continues as leader of the cyclists; he has now assumed the title of Commander.

The death of Sonny (see reports #42, #43) has been without any reprisals; also, Grogan assigned several who had accompanied Sonny on his fatal expedition to various work details around the town area. Though there has been much verbal disagreement with this action, no confrontations have occurred and at this point in time it seems unlikely that this will occur.

Marriette Gaines continues to stay at the StarChild ashram; procedures set forth in the HQ A/P report have been implemented and are in full preparation should their activation become necessary.

Revision is hereby requested on the HQ A/P on Eddy (Edward) Gaines, based on the following:

Gaines appears to have penetrated my cover identity, in a general sense; i.e., he has no hard evidence but his suspicions have been aroused (apparently as a result of previous contact with Federal personnel). His intentions have been stated in monitored correspondence (see copy, Enclosure #A). As will be noted from the text, Gaines poses no immediate or direct threat; it would, however, be beneficial to operations to have Gaines' revised A/P as soon as possible.

Dr. Michelson has made only one further visit to StarChild since my previous report, to assist in a difficult birth. The physician appears to be in failing health, but this observation has at present no confirming data.

Should HQ Advisory activate secondary in accordance with procedure relating to Eddy Gaines, agent requests holding at Flagstaff for contact by standard cut-out procedures.

TRANSMITTAL: CODELEX/COMSAT 22/IAA PRIORITY

XXVIII

chien: development

She sat, bare legs against the cool earth of the dry creek bed, and watched the children. Joan and Sara had gone to Los Caballos; now, for this little while, four-year-old Craig and five-year-old David were *her* family. An illusioned microcosm of what had become only a larger illusion.

For days she had tried to shake off the feeling that she was somehow connected to an unknown future; that she was plummeting down a specific well of Fate with no idea of what might be at the bottom.

The fragile girl, pale blonde hair, blue eyes, might well have been an Alice: *Down, down, down—would the fall* never *come to an end?*

It would have to; Jill *knew* it would have to; falling, she was in limbo. No longer could she touch others, nor could they touch her; for the Fate that had marked her swept her with a blind purpose, and they seemed not to be a part of it. Only with the children did anything seem real.

Why was that?

Perhaps because the children still moved through a world she had left not too long before, a world she could understand though she might not reenter it except in fleeting moments of play. This the yang to the yin all else had become.

Within her, still: the lock.

Pulsing, tidal; answering to the key of a name she did not yet know. In symbols she could only vaguely apprehend: *a lock without a key is not a lock but a seal of metal. This your being holds a lock, Fate promises; promises also that somewhere in another limbo moves the key.*

Craig, with a stick. "It's a magic wand and you're the witch and I come in and I want to be a horse so you change me." With her wave of the wand the boy was gone; in his place the huge muscular horse, limbs glossy. It turned proudly and galloped away along the stones on the hooves of the child's magic, and Jill saw what his mind felt.

And wished the horse could gallop for as many moments in her world as in Craig's. For then the world of the horse would be real.

And the world through which she fell would not be.

XXIX

t'ung jen: fellowship with men

FADE IN:

Day—Cave Interior—Long Shot

We are looking toward the cave entrance, where moving figures are silhouetted by the glare, from far within the cave. We are at the rear of a sizable vaulted cavern, the floor of which slopes up toward the front. SEVERAL CYCLISTS and their motorcyles are visible.

CUT TO:

Day—Cave Interior—Medium Shot

Two or three cycles, parked against the cave wall. We PAN along the wall, passing a dozen cycles; some are being worked on. The camera stops and holds on BEN REED, his cycle, and a man of about thirty, wearing denim pants; this MECHANIC wears no shirt or footwear. He is shaking his head.

CUT TO:

Day—Cave Interior—M.C.U.

Part of the cycle's driveshaft assembly. The shaft itself is in two pieces. The mechanic's hand enters the frame.

> Mechanic's Voice (over)
> Don't know where I can get another one.

CUT TO:

Ben—M.C.U.

> Ben
> What about that BMW you said was smashed up? What about the shaft on that?

CUT TO:

Mechanic—Angle over Cycle—C.U.
>   Mechanic
>   That's still out in the open down there.
>   Kind of a risky proposition.

CUT TO:

Ben—M.C.U.
>   Ben
>   Let me sweat that. You just tell me
>   where it is.

Camera PANS DOWN to the broken driveshaft and
holds as we

DISSOLVE TO:

Drive Shaft Assembly—M.C.U.
Matching the previous shot, except that now the
driveshaft has been moved slightly and is in one piece.
Mechanic's hands come into frame and pick up the
shaft.

QUICK DISSOLVE TO:

Cycle—M.C.U.
A coverplate is being screwed on.

QUICK DISSOLVE TO:

Cycle—Another Angle—C.U.
Wiring is being checked.

QUICK DISSOLVE TO:

Cycle—Headlight—C.U.
The headlight is covered with a protective grille which
would direct the beam downward. SOUND of the
engine starting is heard, and we REVERSE ZOOM to
show Ben sitting on cycle, the mechanic beside him.
>   Mechanic
>   Hey, now, don't you go gettin' your-
>   self killed or busted. I don't wanna see
>   my work goin' all for nothin' . . . y'hear?

Ben gives him a thumbs-up and rolls forward out of
frame.

CUT TO:

Day—Cave Entrance—Exterior—Medium Long Shot
Ben rides out at full speed, doing a small leap over a

rise at the entrance. Camera follows as he does skidding turn and rides down the steeply slanted hill toward dirt road visible at one side of frame. The dust rises from his path, and we ZOOM FORWARD into the cloud of dust as we

FADE OUT

XXX
hsien: influence

A lot of you people out there have been pelting this columnist with various missives to the effect that wasting all my venom on the escapist adventures shows is akin to using a piledriver to crack open a peanut.

So this week I'm going to get you even more annoyed; I'm going to get *really* escapist.

I'm going to talk about 3V news shows.

If you think that all you need for a trip into fantasyland is a few old flatvee *Avengers* or *Prisoner* tapes and whatever joy your shadow pharmacist can dispense, you've been missing a bet.

For the offense, Exhibit A: Don Westrin.

I'd like to think that such phenomena as Westrin are peculiar to what's left out here of Tinseltown (and when was the last time any of you saw tinsel? Just a thought, just a thought)—or to such dark entities as the Center-Fuzz chemical boys; but I have the spooky feeling he isn't. Watch him.

Watch him, and try to get past the super-imposition flag, there even when it isn't (oh yeah: if you don't believe they're still trying that tired old subliminal crap, get a high-resolution VTR and run the tape back at a quarter-speed—the flagflash isn't *all* they use, but you won't believe some of the other stuff unless you see it.) Try to get past the blatantly illegal use of the Center-Fuzz shield on the front of the lectern, to remind us of his former glories as superchief, as if we could ever get past them.

Try, even, if you can without breaking something inside you, to get past the sloganeering and listen to what the man *says*.

It'll scare the shit out of you.

What we've got here is not a failure to communicate, but Westrin doesn't communicate *news*. No; the program boys at KEGL/LA have carefully bracketed Westrin's slot, front and back, with the local and network news. So what they've got is a "news" show with nothing on it to say, unless . . .

. . . unless it's not really a news show at all. Unless it's a thirty-minute admin/establishment hype. If that's what it is, even this far-from-humble reporter has to admit · that Westrin is doing for demagoguery what Olivier and Redgrave used to do for Shakespeare.

Beautiful stuff, friends, beautiful stuff; even the commercial breaks are three-stack sandwiches—the middle one pays the rent, in between public service spots keyed to whatever hobbyhorse his script calls for the old Westrin hero to ride.

Today, a case in point: his report of CenterFuzz coming down on SeaBear commune, up the coast. They were crazed on acid, folks, and plotting all sorts of insidious action against what's left of the State (*what's left*—I use that phrase a lot, these days). Yeah, well, anyway—as if they hadn't busted the place up enough last time, nearly totaled it—the boys in green did a complete wipeout of the place on this go-round.

And all to protect us from those violent acidheads who would've murdered us in our beds. How do we know they would have done that? Simple: the lead-in spot to Westrin's little toe-dance on that atrocity told us so.

And then, in case some of the two-and-three-syllable words in the spot went over our heads, Westrin told us again. Did you know that D-lysergic acid diethylamide tartrate 25 is not only hallucinogenic but unpatriotic? Fact—at least as Westrin presents it.

Just one thing, tapping away back there in my Seven Dwarfs' mine of a brain:

Who's Westrin's audience?

Not *them*. Not the urbos who actually watch it. They already *know* everything he's going to say; it's their Fundamentalist political gospel—and you can't convert the converted.

And certainly not *us*—unless we can't find an old SmoBro reel and get desperate for dadaist amusement. For one thing, we're beyond redemption. For another, we either can't afford or don't want most of the stuff hucksters between Westrin's miniharangues.

So who's he talking to, hey, people?

The Administration, in case he should ever want his old job back?

Posterity? (And I don't even want to *think* about that one.)

Not that Westrin's an anomaly—and in that lies his value, and the reason for these patterings.

Don Westrin is a symbol of a medium that hasn't talked to anybody for a long time—even when it could have, if it had fought to do so. Phosphor-dot, laser-intersect; shadowplay of the lemmings who sold out before they were asked.

Only thing about Westrin is that he's a more obvious example than the rest.

> —*ONE MOMENT PLEASE: A Column Of
> Opinion On Electronic Media By Duane R. Byrd,*
> Phoenix Free Press of Los Angeles
> (date deleted)

hsiao ch'u: taming power of the small

(*It is the best hotel room in the type of vaguely impermanent hotel so often found in the American Southwest. When it was built, some forty years ago, it had possibilities; but all those possibilities have passed it by, and now it is merely a used container for people and furniture. Two windows at the front of the room face out onto the street, but we can see nothing of what might be there, for it is dark now. The curtains of the right-hand window are tinged with red and green from a neon sign outside.*

The room is in a state of general disarray; clothes, beer cans, tools from an opened toolbox are scattered about. The bed is unmade and the mattress is part-way off the bed frame.

The door opens and Trina enters; she flicks on the overhead light, which issues from a dusty plastic chandelier.)

TRINA: Jesus Christ.

(*She surveys the room with loathing. For a moment she considers flopping down on the bed, but it would be too much work to straighten it out first. She drops into an overstuffed chair and puts her knuckles to her eyes.*)

VOICE: Trina? Hey, Trina?

TRINA: In here, Joi. (*Joi enters.*) If you can find a place to sit in all this crap.

(*Trina is only slightly the older of the two girls, at twenty-four; yet there is about her an air of assurance, of knowing exactly who she is, that makes Joi seem much more a child. Yet even this aura, coupled with her manner of dress—cycle jacket, jeans and boots—does not counter the femininity projected by the smoothly modeled features, the green eyes and the luxuriant dark hair. Here, too, Joi's round features and mahogany-brown hair suffer a contrast that makes her babyish by comparison.*)

JOI: Wow. Didn't look like this when we—what d'you suppose they did in here?

TRINA: Fucked a bike, it looks like. Jesus. I really need this. I really need Grogan. If that motherfucker's going to go on his little gung-ho army trip he could sure as hell start here. Get some of his little buck privates up here.

(*Joi picks her way across the room and finds a clear spot on the edge of the bed. As she does so Trina sits up and wriggles out of the leather jacket. Underneath she is wearing a thermal-net t-shirt—and, in a belt-mounted holster, a .32 automatic pistol.*)

JOI: When did they say they'd be back? I thought—
TRINA: I don't know. Motherfucker.
JOI: What're you so uptight about?

(*Trina is silent for a time; she takes a joint from a small pouch at her throat, lights it, inhales, holds.*)

JOI: (*Cautiously. She is Trina's friend, but she can never be sure just what that means.*) I mean, Grogan does this all the time, doesn't he? Why's now so different?

TRINA: (*exhales*) Now not so different. Me different. Me thinking. I don't know if it means anything, but somebody told me that a cat I knew a while ago is heading this way. I think about him, and then I look around at all this shit, and I guess I start comparing what might be could be with what I got, and come up on the short end. Grogan can be awful beautiful and he can be a shit. And he just doesn't seem as beautiful as he used to.

JOI: What's his name?

TRINA: The other cat? Ben. Ben Ben Ben. Huh, if he shows up my old man might end up looking downright ugly.

JOI: You better be careful. That could be a bad scene.

TRINA: (*another long hit from the joint*) Could be. Could be. Ben can handle a lot of things—I think he can handle Grogan. And wouldn't I like to see that mother get it, just once, that'd be enough.

JOI: (*She has moved to the window, and is looking down at the street as though the duel had already begun.*) I don't know. I think it could really be a lot of trouble. And no matter who won you could really get fucked over.

TRINA: (*Smiles; Helen of Troy could have worn this smile.*) Oh, I'm planning to get fucked—over—and over and over. Ben. Hurry up and get here, lover. I have plans for us.

(*She unholsters the pistol and ejects the clip; works the slide to eject the round in the chamber; begins to fieldstrip the pistol. The smile is still on her face.*

At the window, Joi turns and watches Trina for a moment; on the younger girl's face is a mixture of fear and admiration. A few seconds pass, and then she turns her face out to the darkness again, eyes intent, as if somewhere out there lay the future, faintly illuminated in the glow of neon.)

XXXII

chia jen: the family

We don't pretend to be perfect.

None of us here at StarChild think we've found the Answer, and we're not about to start shouting that ours is the True Faith and the One Way.

The thing about one-way streets is that they only take you in one direction, and most of us are here because we want to be free to go in *any* direction—or no direction at all.

We're pacifists because we think that nonviolence is the only way that will work *in the long run*. And that phrase is important; we know that a lot of people have been fighting the CenterFuzz with everything from rocks to bombs ever since the Trouble started, and are still just as alive as we are.

But there are two points that have to be borne in mind:

One: We're stationary, and we're a large group. We can't dodge around and hide, disappear into holes in the ground if the heat comes down heavy on us.

Two: We don't *confront* them—CenterFuzz—but you people out there with the hand grenades do. On the one hand, you might think that we're copping out, that we should be on the road with the gasoline bombs and the shotguns, instead of just sitting here and doing our own little number.

On the other hand, we've got reality; and reality says that we came out here because we didn't want to fight a war, either *for* the micomplex or *against* it—that's why we're here to begin with.

Reality also says that if CenterForce ever decides to really come down on us, and the government thinks they can hide it from the rest of the world, *none of us* are going to stand a chance up against their armory. It won't be guerrilla warfare, it'll be scorched earth, and the Free Cities'll just be craters.

So what it is, is that we've reached the stage where pacifism isn't an ideal philosophy with no application; it is simply the only way we can be what we want to be and still have even a slim chance to survive.

—Marc Hammond, *StarChild Bulletin*
Number Eighty-seven: Nonviolence

XXXIII

k'un: the receptive

By now Tex should have been in Marble Fork for several hours—and probably wondering what had happened to him. Yet as Ben rode southward, angling slightly away from the direction of his final destination, he moved with a subconscious caution.

The louvred headlamp sent a pool of light racing ahead, for it was not a combat circumspectness that held him; it was the vivid memory of the shattered driveshaft, the sound it had made.

The cycle was an extension of him, and it had been nearly two years since it had required any extensive repair, and that only because of a direct hit by a Center-Force slug. Ben had begun to think the cycle was invulnerable—and that, therefore, so was he. The sudden and unheralded snapping of the driveshaft had been an icewater reminder of their separate and intertwined mortality.

Luckily, the shaft had broken on the bias, and had been sealed in a bearing cylinder of Ben's own design; it had held for the twenty miles needed to get it to the caves.

A faint smile flickered on Ben's face as he thought of Tex in the Rover; not having the speed to outrun CenterForce on the highway, Tex almost always traveled overland, where the huge buses could not follow. In some situations this was a disadvantage, but the pattern of roads here was such that his straightline route would give excellent time compared to Ben.

But, slightly spooked in a way that he could/would

not really admit, Ben did not want to subject the cycle to an overland route—not at night, not now, so soon after *it* had happened.

Faded signs, brown/rust and gray/metal, told him that off to his left was Zion National Park, but he was not tempted. The roads through the park, even if still passable, would twist and turn in scenic mazes. The quick route was the long one, and he would stay to it.

Trina and Grogan in Marble Fork: so Tex had said. If Grogan were there Ben could expect to find a number of old acquaintances in the mass of bikers that must have followed their leader. Old home week, it would be.

Old home week; and no home.

(*The thought flickered: triggered, faint memories stirred: a conscious swerve, hate-adrenalin: the memories slept.*)

Trina, now. A possibility. Ben had no idea what the bit might be between Grogan and blackhair prettyface body, but she had given Ben the sign; if it was still there things might be very interesting.

That Grogan might pose a threat, that a death might have to occur so he could put his body into Trina's body, was only a faint overlay to Ben's thoughts, a pattern barely above the level of awareness. His mind did not dwell on it.

If Ben had thrown a rock, his mind would not have dwelt on its inevitable fall to earth.

XXXIV

ta kuo: preponderance of the great

INTERNATIONAL MEDIA SERVICES
TR629PM EST
(DATE DELETED)
NEW YORK N. Y.

IN A PREPARED SPEECH GIVEN AT THE MEETING HALL THIS AFTERNOON THE PRESIDENT INDICATED HIS INTENTION OF AUTHORIZING A STUDY OF QUOTE THE GOALS PURSUED BY THE LATE SENATOR THEODORE NORTH, WHICH MAY HAVE IN PART CONTRIBUTED TO THE ATTACK WHICH TOOK HIS LIFE UNQUOTE.

THE CHIEF EXECUTIVE WENT ON TO SAY THAT THIS AUTHORIZATION WAS IN NO WAY INTENDED TO INDICATE ADMINISTRATION APPROVAL OF THE PROGRAMS AND/OR PROCEDURES SET FORTH IN THE SO CALLED QUOTE AMNESTY BILL UNQUOTE, BUT THAT THE ENEMIES OF THE DEMOCRATIC PROCESS MUST BE SHOWN THAT OURS IS NOT A COUNTRY TO BE RUN BY TERRORISTS.

THE STUDY COMMITTEE WHICH WILL EXAMINE THE LATE SENATOR'S PROPOSALS WILL BE APPOINTED AT THE END OF THE YEAR AND WILL BEGIN THEIR DELIBERATIONS IN THE EARLY SPRING, THE PRESIDENT SAID.

RECENTLY BACK FROM VACATION AT AN UNDISCLOSED LOCATION, THE PRESIDENT

LOOKED FIT AND TANNED. THE LIMP FROM THE SHRAPNEL WOUND INFLICTED IN LAST YEAR'S ASSASSINATION ATTEMPT, WHICH NEARLY COST THE CHIEF EXECUTIVE HIS LEFT LEG, IS NOW HARDLY NOTICEABLE. INFORMATION FROM RELIABLE SOURCES INDICATES THE PRESIDENT HAS DISCONTINUED THE USE OF ANALGESIC INJECTIONS FOR THE MOST PART, AND FEELS LITTLE PAIN.
END TEXT
FOR IMMEDIATE USE   GENERAL
REF129PM THIS DATE

XXXV

i: the corners of the mouth

Why are we here?
Why do we dwell on this ball of mud?
Many of us have answers to these questions,
　　or claim to have,
　　often with words like mirrors
　　which deflect back each listener to himself
　　and often with actions
　　which give an answer we would not wish to speak.
One says:
　　I lay up treasure after treasure in a storehouse;
　　you may see the magnitude of my life in the riches
　　which I possess.
Another speaks:
　　I am a leader of men,
　　thousands bow to my will;
　　you may see the magnitude of my life in the many
　　who obey me.
And a third:
　　I am a seeker after facts
　　and know much of the physical world;
　　you may see the magnitude of my
　　　　life in the knowledge
　　I have set down.
Yet what shadowland is this?
　　Do the treasures differ in your vaults
　　　　than in another's?
　　Can those who obey you think other
　　　　thoughts than yours?
　　Will the facts you have gathered be facts tomorrow?

Objects can be moved about
    as can people
    like chesspieces on a board
    and it matters little to the pawn on what
        square he rests
    when he is taken.
There is but one thing we bring with us
    into this world
    which will remain after we are gone.
This is simply
    to love one another
    and to leave behind us when we depart
    the warmth of memory
    in the hearts of those we have loved.
Even this immortality
    though not a fantasy paradise
    is a reason for our moments
    between Limbo and Oblivion.

—lin ho: *Visions On A Mud Ball*
translated by Chester Valentine

XXXVI

t'ai: peace

They were all in Bigdome; hand clasped in hand clasped in hand clasped in a magic bounding their circle.

Jill was linked into the circle; quartile, she had noticed, to Sara, Joan and Marc. This accident of arrangement, if accident it was, had helped; it had made her feel part of a pattern again, part of something that had a greater meaning than her single aloneness.

This was her first time back in the circle in several days, but it was as if she had not been gone. The smiles had the same caring as they had in the past, unshadowed by what had happened. Jill had not wanted to rejoin the circle; for a time it had seemed to her to be a silly and meaningless ritual, as shallow as the services she had attended with her parents—such a short time ago, she realized suddenly—and she had stayed away from Bigdome.

But an ache moved her; an empty lassitude that seemed to strain toward something she knew not; and the needing of it drew her to these people she loved, a needing that took warmth from the handclasps and the gathered energies, and stayed the ache for a time.

Perhaps a part of the StarChild in which she had moved had sat in cloudless fantasy; an unreal projection of her needs which had collapsed at reality's onslaught. Now, again, she must explore the patterns of love and trust; she must find who she is in relation to StarChild, and what it can be in relation to her.

Far above her, at the apex of the dome, its white-and-orange cap of silk flapsnapped in the breeze, gleamed in the sunlight; within, the sectioned walls reflected the ensnared light to the ring of people below.

Then, for a moment, the wind died, and all was silent.

Within the dome, the people of StarChild savored the moment; fingers clasped a little more tightly. Jill closed her eyes and relaxed into the pause in the movement of time.

Within her, still, the lock: waiting.

But now, again, she was not alone; and she could accept the lock—until the time came for it to open.

XXXVII

ch'ien: modesty

FROM: HQ Advisory/Control
TO: Jonathan Gansell/S14 B2a
LOCATION: Marble Fork, Arizona
DATE: (deleted)
CO/P: (deleted)
REFRENCE: Report #45
TEXT: HQ Section has analyzed your latest report; particular attention has been focused on the possible breach of your cover by Eddy (Edward) Gaines.

It is the decision of this section that current Analysis and Policy re Gaines will continue, subject to the following modifications:

1. Should Gaines communicate his suspicions to you directly, you are to remain noncommittal; this event, and any request made by Gaines, are to be reported to this section immediately.

2. Should Gaines make any direct threat of exposure, or attempt to so expose, you are to terminate him with prejudice.

3. Directive in Par. 2 above is to apply to any persons to whom Gaines succeeds in communication of said relevant information; should the number of persons so involved exceed five (5), you are directed to contact this section prior to fulfillment of this directive.

4. This section is also to be contacted before any action is taken, should Gaines inform his daughter (Marriette Gaines).

5. In accordance with Standing Directives, secondary has been activated and will be on standby/hold at Flag-

staff, no later than (date deleted), ten days from this date. You are to contact secondary at earliest opportunity. Order of precedence for cut-out procedure: Three (3), Four (4), Six (6).

TRANSMITTAL: CODELEX/COMSAT 22/CBI PRIORITY

XXXVIII

feng: abundance

. . . and yet, for all my railing and ranting to the empty night, a Beckett character in his proper setting; for all my illusory nostalgia for a world that only exists in the past of my dreams; for all my pessimism concerning a future that can *only* look promising through the veils of fantasy—

—for all this; when, today, I brought Joan's new child into the world, smacked into him that first wondrous intake of breath, heard the first cry of existence of a voice which has never existed before—I thought I had done something good.

What passage now awaits young Joshua, with me at the one end and Charon at the other? What manner of world is his to grow up in—if (I force myself to write the words) he is given the chance to grow?

Will the love that surrounds young Joshua now be enough to wall him off from the princes of death and the masters of war until he can learn to survive for himself? And when he becomes a man, no longer protected by that wall of love, will he, like that other Joshua, be able to bring down the walls of fear and hate that now divide the land he has inherited?

Much speculation over nine pounds, six ounces of humanity; the gropings of an old man to find some purpose in an act beyond the act itself, even when that act is a joyous one.

When I had only Joshua's first few hours of existence, I was born to an America with the seed of greatness within it, and the strength to right its wrongs; somewhere along the path the dream failed. When Joshua has my years, will the promise this land made to my youth be kept?

I must expect that it shall not; but I find that I can still hope that it will.

—from the daily journal of
Dr. M. J. Michelson
(all dates deleted)

XXXIX

chun: difficulty at the beginning

Ben coasted slowly along the street in a pool of shadow only slightly darker than the soft tar on which it glided; the sun sat at the top of the sky, in too-brilliant glare, as though it had something personal against Marble Fork.

There were only a few people visible on the solitary main street, which did not surprise Ben. Now that Marble Fork was a biker town, it would have only two types of people; the bikers, who would only be on the street after dark—and whoever was left of the original population, who would rarely show up on the street for any reason. He had been in a hundred small towns like Marble Fork—and the pattern never varied.

For a split-second after the sound he thought he had blown a tire, but in the same instant the gouge appeared in the tar in front of him. Ben did a backward flip off the cycle, whipping the Winchester out of its sheath as he did so. His mind had registered: *to the right, high angle.*

Even as he tracked to the proper window, a shell going into the chamber, the voice came from within. "Reed, you crazy mother, cool it! I was just messing around."

"I'm not impressed." But he recognized Grogan's voice.

"Oh, come on, man, look at the range. You know damn well I could have dropped you if I'd wanted."

This was perfectly true; Ben had seen Grogan in action.

He thought about how to play it for a second; then, with a faint smile, pulled the trigger. The two windows, in register near the top of the frame, disappeared inward as the sound of the explosion mingled with that of breaking glass and rending wood.

Silence for a few seconds.

"Hey! You crazy motherfucker!"

"It's cowboy time," Ben called out. "Out onto the roof, now, gun by the barrel."

Shamefacedly, Grogan clambered out. He paused to glare at the few others who had stopped on the street or poked their heads out the window to watch. When his gaze finally traveled back to Ben, the shotgun had been reholstered in the again-upright cycle; Ben was laughing. Grogan burst out laughing as well, and swung from a projecting gable down to the street.

"What the fuck'd you wanna do that for? Waste a round, man."

"I could ask you the same question, genius."

Grogan held up the revolver. "No sweat—.38 rounds are easy to get. I must have a couple crates, and every time CenterFuzz loses a bus somebody manages to come by some more. Shit, I don't know where there's any loads for that cannon of yours."

"No big problem, I don't use it that much. Just thought your little greeting called for something or other. I'm nothin' if not polite. Anyway," Ben had spotted a familiar sight, "I can see a place where I can get reloads from where I'm standing."

Grogan glanced around puzzledly, scratching his neat black beard. "What're you talking?"

"The Land Rover, you dumb shit. You nearly landed on it when you came off the roof. Isn't it Tex's?"

The gang chieftain blinked. "Oh. Yeah. Yeah, he's been here for a while. I never even thought about that. Yeah, he can load anything, can't he?"

"Just about."

"Yeah. Well. I'm still a little wasted. Didn't go to sleep until a few hours ago."

"Don't tell me Tex told you I was coming in and you got up special just to give me your .38 caliber welcome."

"No. No, you're not pretty enough. No, my old lady, you remember Trina, she got up for some reason to go someplace and made the same kind of racket she always does."

"I wouldn't know about that."

"I better never catch you learning." For a moment, then, in Grogan's eyes, the *machismo* steel; registered between them; then gone.

"If I ever mess with Trina it'll be on our way back from the cemetery when they bury you."

Grogan laughed. "Only other way will be on your way *to* the cemetery, *amigo*."

Ben wheeled his cycle into a space beside the Land Rover and locked it to a stanchion. "Nothin' against your old lady, man, she's great-looking stuff, but nobody's worth that kind of trip."

"She sure ain't. Y'know I gotta keep up the front, though, if I want to keep running this show."

"I heard in Reno you were chieftain. What happened to whatsisname, Michaels, if you don't mind my asking?"

"Like everybody said would happen. His mouth was just a little too fast for his piece. He gave me some shit, I gave him some shit back, he thought he was gonna snuff me but I thought first. That was a while ago, man, happened right after we got here."

"Any hassles with local heat?"

"Long gone, baby. Just Gaines, cat that runs the bar; he used to be the Sherf, but when we come in he figured it'd be better just to tend a little bar and forget about the badge."

Ben had known Michaels; they had not been friends, not in this world where every friend was a way they could get to you; not friends, but Ben had liked him. "So old Michaels is gone. Anybody hassle it when you took his slot?"

"Not to my face." Grogan's laugh this time was something hard, with glinting edges. "Not behind my back, either, those bastards know what's good for them. Anybody wept for Curly didn't tell me about it."

Ben shifted slightly, to loosen his boot from the soft tar, and wiped the sweat off his forehead with a sleeve. "Boss of this town oughta be able to find me a cold brew."

"No sweat; right inside. Then, m'boy—"

"Then what?"

"Then we'll go find where my old lady's run off to. She'll probably wanna say hello."

XL

meng: youthful folly

Momma love,

I know I haven't written in a while but you shouldn't worry if it's a long time between letters. We just never know when somebody will be coming through that can take them to Flagstaff or someplace where there's a post office.

I did get that package that you gave to Benito and Sue when they stopped by. I got it about five weeks after the date of the letter you had in with the things. Benny and Sue said Daddy came home while they were there and almost wouldn't let them take the package with them. I hope you didn't get into any trouble or arguments with Daddy because of that. It was really nice to have that stuff, it's just been ages since I've worn perfume. I guess I won't wear it long because we share stuff here a lot and those bottles will probably go pretty fast.

From what Benny and Sue said Daddy sounds like he's still the way he was before I left. If only he would *try* to understand maybe he would see it isn't so bad, but it seems like he wants me to live his life all over again instead of mine. Doesn't he know that I couldn't even if I wanted to? The world just isn't like it was when he was as old as I am now. I could tell from your letter that you're worried about me but you don't think I did some terrible evil thing even if it isn't what you wanted me to do.

I was wondering whether or not I should tell you this next part but I guess I will, since it's all over and nothing happened. And it shows maybe I've got a guardian angel over me. Some of the bikers from ~~Marin Park~~ the town near here came out to the ashram. They hit the boy down at the gate and then they came up here where the buildings are. They started talking loud, saying nasty things, and one of them came over and just started saying sick things to me and then he grabbed me. But some other bikers had come in and the one that I think was the leader took the man away from me and hit him. He fell down and didn't move and then the leader apologized to me and the other people here. I ran away and was sick and when I came back later all the bikers were gone. Somebody said that the one who had grabbed me was dead but they took him with them so I don't know.

I know that all sounds bad, but it's like the worst thing that could have happened, and it didn't. I still feel a little strange about it but I'm not really frightened or anything.

Joan had a baby! He's so beautiful and his name is Joshua. There's a doctor in the town and he came out and helped deliver him. I'm staying with Joan now and helping out.

I think Marc is maybe in love with me. I don't know because he's affectionate and gentle with everybody but he seems to be around me a lot. He's nice, and in a way I love him too, but I think maybe like a brother. I know he won't get pushy or anything because that's just not the way he is, but I hope I don't hurt his feelings. If he really *does* feel that way about me.

I love you and Daddy veryvery much. I guess you can't tell Daddy that or he'd know you got the letter and want to read it and then just get mad. Love and Peace

JILL

XLI

k'un: oppression

SECTOR: SW II
FACILITY: DenPeb Internment Central
UNIT OF ORIGIN: CenterForce Patroller J4409
  (direct)
DATE: (deleted)
DETAINEE: John Millard Adams/AKA Hot John
SUPPLEMENTAL: Approx. 30 years of age, 194
lbs., ht. 6'1"; numerous scars, marks and tattoos
ARREST REPORT: Adams traveling south on Intst.
25, was approx. 12 miles north of Colo./New Mex.
border when first seen by J4409. Request to stop, made
by light signal and speaker, ignored by Adams, who
drove his vehicle (cycle) off the highway in attempt to
elude Patroller. Burst fired from forward-mounted X-
AutoTrac disabled vehicle and wounded Adams, who
was rendered unconscious.

Arrested under. Proviso I of Domestic Enemies Act.
CONFINEMENT REPORT: Adams brought directly
to DenPeb IC Receiving by J4409.

After treatment in sick bay for six days Adams
assigned to Barracks S-354, Bay Two.

Altercation with guards resulted in twenty days in
solitary.
INTERROGATION REPORT: Adams was not co-
operative with interrogating officials. Responses to
queries concerning acquaintances, their probable loca-
tions and intentions, generally composed of obscenities
or vilification of DenPeb IC and its officials.

Analysis of medical examination indicates psychopharmacological interrogation procedures would be ineffective with this detainee.

DISPOSITION: Adams placed on Permanent Detention status; subject to review after administration of Psychiatric Modification procedures, and/or following any variance from Behavior Profile.

XLII

chen: the arousing

If it was still there things might be very interesting.

It was still there; if Trina had made it any more obvious either Ben or Grogan might have had to die right then.

But: arms around the neck, "Oh, Ben! When'd you get in?", the split-instant jolt of her tongue in his ear (on the side away from Grogan), and then the step back to the proper distance and set of the body, distance and set that said, for public consumption: *Grogan's girl.*

The public, half a dozen assorteds in the cool gas station garage, was for the most part undeceived. The electric vibrations of trouble moved out in expanding rings; sensed, they were not made the subject of comment but only logged into the table of future expectations. When it happened, in Eddy's or on the street, these people would not be surprised.

The only one deceived was (in accordance with his needs) Grogan; much, of course, as Trina had intended. She knew the hairline borders of his visions and perceptions, his suspicions and his hungers.

And his blindnesses; she danced among them so skillfully that Grogan was unaware she moved at all.

Under the chieftain's beneficent imprimatur Ben made his hellos, passed on some news, anecdotalized his adventures. It would have played well except for the one off-note, the silent regard of Trina. To Grogan it was a rare attentiveness; to the others it was the second cable of the web her greeting had begun to spin; to Ben it was a sense of time and moments that would come, shadow to sunlight to shadow, Trina's warmth beneath him in a place he did not yet know, Grogan's eyes and voice in bloodrage and the stubby metal hole that would try to spit oblivion into him.

But whatever pattern of Ben's future this might be, these vague images, he himself saw them only as possible/probable events, having no more to do with him directly than might the words scrawled on the wall of a corridor through which he passed.

That he was at all involved with, had anything to do with, the events that intersected his life-sequence: this was a notion that might have occurred to him, but only as a misty speculation—and Ben was not much given to speculation.

You don't *do* things—you just *live*—and things happen to you.

Think little about the future, and less about the past.

It is not a mystic predestination; it is simply that the *world* has free will—and it is the world and its hidden intentions which moves you, Ben Reed, along a path as far as your straining gaze—

—and no farther.

XLIII

pi: grace

There are many kinds of holiness,
     many avenues to transcendence.
There is the recluse,
     stylite, hermit, ascetic,
     desert-wanderer,
     who forsakes the world of man
     and all his works.
There is the mystic,
     trance-bound, symbol-webbed,
     who forsakes the man
     who is himself.
There is the churchman,
     whose occupation it is
     to supply his god
     to the proper supplicants,
     who forsakes all direct experience,
     and moves on step by step.
There is the evangelist
     who spreads his own direct experience
     thinly over thousands.
There are as many visions of holiness
     as are there personal visions
     of something beyond our existence.
Can it be said a given path is wrong or right?
Or only that *no* given path can be
     the *only* wrong—
     the *only* right?

Is it not true that,
      as we can never truly experience the
         mind of another,
      so also their personal vision of Transcendence
      can never be fully shared?
And if this is so:
      that it matters not
      what path one takes to holiness,
      but only the path
      on which one travels to find it,
      through the lives of others.
If you would know
      that the Tree you climb
      is the One Tree of Life and Enlightenment,
      you have only to look
      at what this Tree of your existence bears.
By your fruit
      shall you know yourself.

              —lin ho: *Visions On A Mud Ball*
              translated by Chester Valentine

XLIV

k'uei: opposition

(*Eddy's Bar. Were it not for the electric fixtures, the aged but serviceable Wurlitzer at the rear of the large room, it might well be a saloon of a hundred years ago— or, at least, a set for one, built for a low-budget Hollywood western. The bar top, the tables are clean; the floor has not been swept in several days. A blue-tinted mirror, in four sections, is mounted behind the bar; the section nearest the swinging doors is shattered, a sunburst of lines running out from some object's point of impact.*

It is late afternoon. There are no customers at the bar behind which Eddy Gaines stands, and only three of the tables are occupied; two, near the entrance, with assorted members of Grogan's group—and the third, at the rear of the room near the Wurlitzer, with Ben Reed, Terry Grogan, Trina Gordon and Tex Gernicke.

The table is littered with several beer cans and two wine bottles.)

(*Grogan is speaking.*)

GROGAN: So I was just getting tired of dodging those shits all the time, and when old Michaels told me about this deal I didn't figure it'd hurt to look.

BEN: And after you took the look you snuffed him.

GROGAN: Yeah, well, like I said, he had a little too much mouth on him. Fucking *cabron*, who cares?

TRINA: *Cabron*, eh? He let you make it with Jennie? Funny you never told me about that.

GROGAN: Oh Jesus. You know what I mean.

BEN: So who else you been putting down?

GROGAN: Sonny, for one.

TEX: Oh, come on, man, that little clown?

GROGAN: He went out to that hippie layout. Figured to get hisself some little fresh bush. So I went out and just cold-cocked him. N'he didn't get up, that's all.

BEN: What've they got, some special privileges out there, they're holy or something?

TEX: No, man. It was a discipline thing.

GROGAN: You got it. Let 'em get away with one fucking thing and pretty soon it's somebody else is giving the orders. I didn't really think I was going to waste him permanent with one punch like that, man. Hell, if that's all it took maybe it's better that way.

TRINA: What the fuck are you talking about? You a psycho or something?

(*The pause is a mild electric waiting; the woman never calls down on her man in front of other men; not in the world through which these people move. Trina senses that perhaps she has gone too far almost as soon as the words are out of her mouth, but she is too arrogant to make any moves toward retraction.*)

GROGAN: (*after the pause*) Seems like I was just talking about people that get put down because they have too much mouth.

(*Trina's eyes flash something which she is too smart to put into words—right now, at least.*)

TEX: Well, Sonny wasn't anything much to worry about, but I have to say that Curly Michaels is better off where he is—wherever *that* is. You ever see that thing somebody wrote about him in *Phoenix*, the L.A. paper? Poem called *Bloodbird?*

(*Ben and Grogan shake their heads.*)

Really pegged him. Must have been one of the chicks he fucked over wrote it; that cat was a walking disaster area, just find out where the chick—or a guy, for that matter—find out their weak spot and zing right in on it. I never figured he was going to go of old age. I see Jennie's with Brian now, and she sure looks a hell of a lot better.

BEN: What is this hippie place you went to?

GROGAN: They call it StarChild, got the name out of some movie I think. They're pretty cool, they don't lay their trip on us and we don't hassle them. Wouldn't be much point—they don't have anything much out there, and even if they did and we wanted it they wouldn't fight or anything. It'd be like robbing little kids.

TEX: Hear about Hot John?

BEN: How could I hear anything? I only just got in.

TEX: Busted. They've got him in the camp up in Colorado. Ain't that a kick in the ass?

BEN: (*after a pause*) Shit. We've got to get him out of there.

GROGAN: Sure you do. What're you gonna do, hire the Air Force to bomb the place?

TEX: It's never been done. Course I don't think anybody's been crazy enough to try it.

GROGAN: You motherfuckers are *both* crazy.

TRINA: You'll just give them two more, probably dead at that.

BEN: I don't know, man. (*to Tex*) How about it, my man? You game to run a number on good ol' CenterFuzz?

TEX: Wow, baby, you know it really *is* crazy. They'd never expect it, would they?

BEN: No. And if we proved it *could* be done, maybe a lot more cats would try.

TRINA: Fanfuckingtastic. You're serious.

TEX: Why not? I mean, you know: because it is there.

GROGAN: Do me one favor. Leave anything you don't need here. Better we should inherit it than Center-Fuzz.

BEN: Just so you don't use it before we get back.

TRINA: Listen, if you're really going to do this, maybe you should take a run out to StarChild first. The guy that runs the place, they've got his younger brother in there and he managed to get a couple of letters out to him. Maybe he'll know something.

BEN: Yeah, but would he talk to us?

TRINA: Oh, fuck, man, beat it out of him!

TEX: Little old blood 'n guts, aren't you, sweets? Do let me point out to you that it's not always such a great idea to get information that way, especially if wrong information will kill you dead enough so you don't come back to complain. It's an old rule. But we can give him a try, see where his head's at.

GROGAN: Anything I can get you for this little suicide special?

BEN and TEX: (*simultaneously*) Mortars.

(*All four laugh.*)

GROGAN: Eddy! Bottle of wine for the Suicide Squad.

XLV

ta ch'u: taming power of the great

(EXTRACT FROM CORRO MANUSCRIPTS/FRAG. 91b)

. . . (through?) many prior Administrations that such internment camps were not being repaired and reactivated on a standby basis, subsequent events proved the falsity of such official statements.

That the passage of the Domestic Enemies Act (q.v.) gave impetus to the reactivation of the camps, and that this process was accelerated by the creation of the CenterForce agency, cannot be denied. However, much more important (in the humble opinion of this historian) was a particular psychological climate which had existed since the middle Fifties, and which had deepened markedly as the years passed.

One popular term for this mental outlook was "polarization": an invisible fence which divided those who accepted the country as it was (generally white, older generation, middle class or higher) from those who wished to change the ways and direction of the country, either by democratic process or by revolutionary action (generally minority groups, the poor, students). At the time this polarization was first noted as a social phenomenon, most commentators seemed to think that, of these groups, the least likely to be affected was the white middle class.

The rationale was that, as this group was generally conservative and would tend toward an isolationist view if any stress was put upon their socioeconomic position, members of this class would tend to treat views at variance with their own as those of a lunatic fringe. Any indications of numerical strength for these opposition views (the theory presumed) would be discounted as the fabrications of corrupted news media.

This theory was reinforced by the postulation by one Administration of a "Silent Majority." The idea of this was apparently *those who are not against us are for us*. It is, of course, true that under any government, at any time through history, criticism of the controlling group will be confined to a relatively small number, since few citizens tend to involve themselves in political questions (except in those countries which hold elections, and even in such situations, that segment of the population which votes is in most cases completely ignorant of both candidates and issues).

One major point eluded the analysts of the time, however, and for this reason they were unable to predict the gradual breakdown of the middle and upper middle class as a government-oriented bloc.

This was, put simply, the American tradition: a set of beliefs instilled in most older members of this bloc from their earliest years. This tradition pictured the United States as the last bastion of religious and intellectual freedom in the world, and all of the symbols central to its existence—the Statue of Liberty, the Declaration of Independence, the Liberty Bell, the Constitution, to name only the most obvious—tended to reinforce this concept. It ran far deeper than a mere political concept; this feeling that America, perhaps alone, let any citizen speak as he pleased, to his leaders or to his God, was the emotional base of something which was not jingoism, nationalism or patriotism—but a simple and almost romantic love of country.

If we view them in this light, we can see that their reaction to the Administrations which created such things as the DE Act and the reactivated internment camps was the reaction of a man whose lover has been insulted. Only the existence of such a reaction can explain their sudden *en masse* departure from enlightened

self-interest, and subsequent transformation within a
decade from the defenders of the status quo to but another segment of the oppressed—though they were,
perhaps, its elite.

The Camps

Six Internment Centers had been activated when the
program was in full operation; of these, only two were
located east of the Mississippi River—outside the cities
of Perth Amboy, New Jersey, and Charleston, South
Carolina. Though this distribution would seem at variance with population figures, these two installations were
in their final form several times larger than those in the
western part of the country.

These latter were located near Crystal City, Texas;
between Denver and Pueblo, Colorado; Omaha, Nebraska; and Portland, Oregon. Personnel to man the
camps were drawn from various government agencies
on a draft basis; because of this, morale of guards and
officials of the camps was generally low.

Physical layout of the camps, and subsequent security,
varied greatly since no firm policy had been established;
those in the East tended toward an amalgam of prison
and military stockade, while the western installations
followed for the most part the pattern of the Internment
Camps used to detain Japanese-Americans during the
Second War.

Control of the prisoners (or Detainees, as they were
sometimes called) was accomplished by a combination
of traditional methods with those of pharmacology and
behavior modification. In some extreme cases psycho-
surgery (lobotomy) was employed; detainees who received this treatment were often subsequently released
into the general population. Their condition, however,
in the context of the times, did not tend in the direction of survival.

Such fragmentary data as are available seem to indicate that many radical medical and psychological
techniques were used in effecting . . .

XLVI

hsieh: deliverance

Evening: iron, rubber, painted metal/chromed metal, it stood near the entrance to Bigdome. Reflections of distant firelight and lanternglow, caught in the webbed mirror of the spokes. She had thought (it now occurred to her) that after what had happened she might be afraid of bikers, even the cycles alone; no.

Not, at least, with this one. She had heard the sound of the engine, waited until it stopped; then had left Joan and Joshua to satisfy her curiosity—to test her fear.

And there had been no fear. Even with the gun in the long holster, it was not a roaring monster, coated with death and violence. It was—only a machine. Something that waited, like a horse or a dog. A—

No.

It was none of these things, for it seemed incomplete. Not like a part was missing (Jill would not have known if it were), but as though the cycle were part of something else. Of course the feeling made no sense.

The other part stepped out from the Bigdome entrance; the part looked at her across the rough ground.

In the center of her being: a lock of sea-rough metal. Now, in this instant, it was the nucleus, the ylem from which her universe had sprung. Who Are*You Are You Are*You? In the center of the lock: her being. Through fading sea-rough metal, the land and the stars; still there, still waiting for her tomorrows.

Ben saw her.

In-credible. And here he'd been planning to mess with

Trina, do that whole big bad number and all that hassle; and who knew what was going on in Trina's head? But that seemed awfully surface now, yeah, Grogan could keep his problem.

Palepale blonde blue eyes ivory skin little sleeveless shift bare arms legs barefoot. She was so *little*. One hand could break her, could crush her; no hand would. Memory: Glenda, Amy, the possibility of Trina, all the others—whitesheet beds, carseats, dirty mattresses, grass, tenement hallway—recall moved, visions shattered; only the image of first-Glenda remained, standing in a shadowed corridor of his mind, seeing through his eyes and filtering them to contrast the essences of the pale princess.

Pale. *Question: Arizona sunlight—how is she so light, why—*

—answering Question, fear-edged: is she real?
Find out. Find out.

"Hiyo."

"Hello."

"We came out—we're looking for the boss, Marc, uh, whatever. You know where we can find him?"

"Marc's over at the North Pen, I think. It's not far, or you can wait for him. He should be back in a few minutes. You're with somebody?"

"Guy named Tex."

"I only see your motorcycle."

"He packed with me. We didn't want to waste gas and I didn't want to leave the bike in town. How do you know it's mine?"

"I don't know, it just seems like it should. I mean, it looks like you. I guess that sounds silly."

"No. Sounds right. You see things good. Yeah, Tex is in your council hogan, I guess it is. You show me where this pen is?"

"Why—why do you want to see Marc?"

"Ho there. Easy. We just heard that he knows something about the big slammer up north and a buddy of ours is there. That's all. Why the big thing?"

"I'm sorry. I mean, I didn't think you were bad or anything, but some other people came out here on bikes, and beat up Jimmie, and one of them was—was going—"

"Whoa. Cool now, I heard about it. Must have been a bad scene. Sure as hell a bad scene for Sonny."

"The one who—did you know him?"

"Kind of. I don't know if you feel bad about that or not, but don't. He was the kind of cat if it hadn't happened here, with Grogan, would have happened someplace else sooner or later. You want to take me to see Marc?"

Evening, in the few minutes, had become night; stars and stars, but the moon had not yet risen. Past the outer ring of structures, a near-black that gave subtle hints of the terrain. In the distance, a kerosene red-lantern hung from a fence crosspiece to mark their destination. Jill knew the path; she took Ben's hand to lead him.

At the moment of contact, they both stood motionless for a moment, though neither knew why.

Over the rough ground, under the stars; no words, but an awareness of each other's presence that was like a physical pain.

When they reached the pen, there was no sign of Marc. Jill called out; no answer, except from one of the goats. In a while someone would be out to do the night watch, sitting on the sleeping bag in the small milking pen and perhaps trying to read by the dim crimson light.

"We must have passed him coming out."

"Don't see how, pretty one. We would've heard him. Maybe he went someplace else."

"He might have come back early, while I was inside. I guess we should go back—"

"Mmn. Not yet."

"Your friend—"

"Tex'll keep."

"Please. Don't."

"*Novia*, don't be scared. I won't do anything you don't want me to. Promise. What's your name, pretty one?"

"Jill."

"Jill. I'm Ben. Not going to hurt you. Okay? Not frightened?"

"Not of you."

"What, then?"

"I don't know. Me, maybe."

"*Por que*?"

"I don't *know*. I never saw you before a little while ago, but—I suppose you must have a lot of girlfriends."

"No. Not any more. You know, just I'll meet somebody and maybe we'll ball but it doesn't mean anything. You, pretty one?"

"I never have, not like that."

"Virgin?"

"It just—just never happened, that's all."

"Wow. Amazing."

"Why is it so—"

"You're just so pretty, *novia*. Like a dream."

"What's that mean—*novia*?"

"Puerto Rican. Means *sweetheart*."

"Do you always say that?"

"No, I—that's funny. I guess I never said that to anybody before."

XLVII

sun: decrease

AGENT: Jonathan Gansell/S14 B2a
LOCATION: Marble Fork, Arizona
DATE: (deleted)
COVER OPERATION/PROCEDURE: (deleted)
REPORT NO.:   51
TEXT: Operational climate at this location remains stable.

Terry Grogan remains in his position as leader of the cyclists; there have been no attempts, either by overt or covert means, to oust him from this position.

There have also been no overtures from Eddy (Edward) Gaines, either to this agent or to any other individual, regarding his suspicions concerning my true identity. As noted in a previous report, revised HQ A/P procedures have been readied for activation when/ if necessary.

Two visitors to the town were identified as Tex Gernicke (not on file: veh. modif. Land Rover) and Ben Reed (fugitive/wam 1554: veh. modif. BMW R60 mc). Conversation established Reed as a possible rival for Grogan both as (a) leader of the cyclists and (b) companion to Trina Gordon, Grogan's present mistress.

However, both visitors departed within thirty-six hours of their arrival. My source at the StarChild ashram states that the two men visited there for a few hours on the evening of Reed's arrival; purpose of the visit was not known. Another report, unverified, indicates that Reed and Gernicke obtained light field weapons of undisclosed type prior to their departure. Probable destination is not known.

HQ A/P requested on Reed and Gernicke in the event they should return to this location.

TRANSMITTAL: CODELEX/COMSAT 22/IAA PRIORITY

XLVIII

huan: dispersion

INTERNATIONAL MEDIA SERVICES
TR210PM EST
(DATE DELETED)
NEW YORK N. Y.
 ADMINISTRATION SPOKESMEN CONFIRMED
TODAY THAT NATIONAL ELECTIONS MAY BE
AGAIN DEFERRED IF RESULTS OF A POSTAL
PLEBISCITE CONFIRM THE PREDICTIONS OF
ADMINISTRATION ANALYSIS.
 CITING THE DIFFICULTIES WHICH REN-
DERED TWO PREVIOUSLY SCHEDULED NA-
TIONAL ELECTIONS UNFEASIBLE, MEETING
HALL PRESS SECRETARY BERNARD THOMAS
NOTED THAT QUOTE WE WILL OF COURSE
FOLLOW THE WISHES OF OUR CITIZENRY,
WHATEVER THOSE WISHES MAY BE UN-
QUOTE, BUT ADDED THAT THE ADMINISTRA-
TION HAD EVERY EXPECTATION THAT THE
PUBLIC WOULD BACK ITS POLICY.
 IN RESPONSE TO A QUESTION REGARDING
SECURITY OF THE PLEBISCITE RETURNS AND
WHAT STEPS MIGHT BE TAKEN TO PREVENT
TAMPERING WITH THE RESULTS, PRESS SEC-
RETARY THOMAS SAID THE QUERY SMACKED
OF MUCKRAKING AND WAS UNDESERVING OF
AN ANSWER.
 THOMAS SAID ALSO THAT THE CHIEF EX-
ECUTIVE WOULD NOT BE AVAILABLE FOR
COMMENT OR MEDIA QUESTIONS AT THIS

TIME, BUT THAT THERE WAS LITTLE DOUBT
THAT THE PRESIDENT WOULD GO ON NA-
TIONAL ALL-NETWORK BROADCAST TO AN-
NOUNCE THE RESULTS OF THE POSTAL
PLEBISCITE.
END TEXT
FOR IMMEDIATE USE   GENERAL
NOREF

XLIX

kuai: breakthrough

FADE IN:

Day—Internment Camp—Long Shot

Ben and Tex are lying prone on the precipice edge of a high ridge. We are looking past them toward, in the far distance, DenPeb Internment Central. From this range, we can make out little except rows of barracks and occasional towers. Tex is studying the scene through binoculars.

CUT TO:

Day—Camp—Medium Shot—Binocular View (Matte)

We PAN slowly back and forth. Now we can see the barbwire-and-chain-link double line of fencing, and the signs which warn that the fence is electrified. The main gate has a tower at either side; we can see two men on duty in each tower, and in each tower a mounted machinegun.

There is a whirr-whine of a small electric motor as we ZOOM in past the fencing and begin to PAN along the barracks.

> Tex's Voice (over)
> Yeah. Pretty much the way he described it. The setup should work if we can get the timing right. What'd he say the barracks number was?

We continue panning the barracks.

> Ben's Voice (over)
> S three-fifty-four. Should be over on the left. Can you see it?

We pan to the left, past the correct barracks, and

then pan back to one end of it. We see a large white square of board, mounted above one of the rudimentary porches, which bears the designation S-354.

> Tex's Voice (over)
>
> Got it! And right in position, too.

CUT TO:

Day—Ben and Tex—Medium Close Shot

> Ben
>
> Now the only thing to worry about is whether John is gonna be in position too. You think that message will get to him?
>
> Tex
>
> Oh, I think so. I think I put the fear of whatever god he believes in into that little intern. He knows if he *doesn't* get that message to John, or gives it to anyone else, that he better never come out of there.

CUT TO:

Day—Internment Camp—Long Shot

Same as first shot of scene.

> Ben (wild track)
>
> Yeah. Well. Gonna be a fun night.

DISSOLVE TO:

Night—Internment Camp—Long Shot—(Time-Lapse Shot)

All is brightly lit within the camp; darkness outside. At some point during the time lapse after sunset, Ben and Tex have disappeared.

CUT TO:

Night—Gully—Medium Shot

We are in a gully on the opposite side of the road from the fence. Down the road we can see the two towers of the main gate. Ben is holding three bundles of dynamite sticks, three sticks to a bundle. Tex is adjusting the angle for the two mortars.

> Ben
>
> How do you know you'll be able to hit *both* towers? Seems like pretty fancy

shooting for that kind of equipment.
Tex
I was taught by the best.
Ben
And who might that be?
Tex
(*nods toward the camp*)
Why, our dear ole gummint, who else?
Ah, who'da thunk it, way back then?
Ben
(*checks his watch*)
Any time you're ready, Doc Holliday.

CUT TO:

Night—Main Gate—Medium Long Shot

There is a four-beat pause. Then suddenly there are two explosions at the base of the towers, which begin to buckle and collapse into the entranceway.

CUT TO:

Night—Road—Long Shot

Looking past the collapsing towers. Three more explosions along the double line of fencing in quick succession. There are sirens, whistles—all hell seems to be breaking loose. We can dimly see a figure racing through the rents in the fence even before the fragments of earth and sand have begun to descend. The figure drops out of sight into the gully.

DISSOLVE TO:

Day—Country Road—Medium Shot

The Land Rover and the BMW are rolling along side by side; a cloud of dust billows out behind them. In the Rover is a passenger, a man of nearly Tex's size.

Hot John (wild track)
So what'd you go to all that trouble for, anyhows? Just to see my smiling face?
Tex (wild track)
We look like sentimental types? No. Ole Reed there says you owe him for a beer.

FADE OUT

L

sung: conflict

Two girls:
She would sit, with Joan and Sara, in the pool of
tinted light beneath Bigdome's roof. They would sew,
hours passing, repairing a tent or dome covering, or the
worn clothing of the children of StarChild. At other
times they would sit with the other women of the
ashram at the shaded tables behind the pantry-cabin,
peeling and chopping vegetables.

Several days had passed; Joan and Sara knew of Ben's
visit, and its effect on Jill—but the young girl had made
no mention of what had happened between them.

It was hardly necessary.

Within her, now, no lock of mindclenched darkness;
no wall of magic to set her apart and away from the
rest of life. That sea-rough metal nexus, with its coldness that could not be felt but sensed—replaced now,
though only a part of this could she yet sense, by a
nucleus of warmth.

Within her, now, life: growing.

She would stand, alone, in the shadows of the domes,
or out at the barren edges of the StarChild land. She
would write, from time to time, scraps of poetry—which
she would as quickly destroy. This destruction was not
the act of a specific hatred, but rather a function of a
general loathing and fanatic disgust with what she was
and what she had been made to be.

Her mother: dead, and perhaps (*said her coldness*) it

was better so. Martha could not have—would not have wanted to—survive what the world had become.

Her father: playing at plots, trying to walk around in the badge-wearing shell of what he had been, a shell now too large for him. Behind his bar, a servant to those he said he hated, copping out now on even his own sick fantasies.

She had been at StarChild for some time now, and it seemed that those few people who knew her father had been the Sheriff of Marble Fork didn't seem to care one way or the other; they didn't seem to connect what other people were with what *she* was, the way her father had done for as long as she could remember.

But, though they had accepted her, she could not accept herself; she was cut off from them by her own feelings about what she was—and had been.

This wall was not of the kind, like Jill's, to be shattered into fragments of fading memory by the gentle beginnings of love. Love, in fact, was a part of this wall; the boy from that college, down Phoenix way, the gold pin, her father standing above them like the avenging angel . . .

. . . no escape through love, through caring; no escape from her father's shadow.

In the shadowed corner of her living space, she gathered up the few things she would take back to town. This hadn't worked, but maybe if she could get away, really far away?

The rest of them were at dinner when she made her way down to the main road; at the gate, she exchanged a mournful nod for Jimmie's questioning shrug. Beyond the town, beyond the low ridge; stars, just faintly visible. If she walked toward the stars perhaps it would not seem so far to the town.

Somewhere, in the distance: a sound of engines.

LI

i: increase

AGENT: S14 B2a
LOCATION: #MF, SW II
DATE: (deleted)
TO: S14 C2b
LOCATION: #FGSTF, SW II
CO/P: (deleted)
TEXT: As provided for in HQ A/P response to my
#45, you are hereby activated as secondary on full
operational status. You will report to me on arrival this
location ASAP.

Refer to your greensheets of my reports for backup
information.

On (date deleted), while returning, apparently, from
the StarChild ashram where she had been staying,
Marriette Gaines was set upon by cyclist or cyclists unknown and repeatedly raped. During the course of this
group assault she was severely injured and put in a
state of shock. For two days she has been under the
constant care of Dr. Michelson, from whom it has been
learned that her condition is critical, intermingling
brief periods of consciousness with longer periods of
semi-comatose sleep.

In spite of the demands of her father, Dr. Michelson
has not permitted him to question his daughter as to
the identities of those who attacked her.

Gaines (the father) has not attempted to contact this

agent at this point; it is essential that you be in place by the time such a confrontation occurs.

TRANSMITTAL: CODELEX/WEB #6/ /COPY/ COMSAT 22/IAA PRIORITY

LII

kuei mei: the marrying maiden

Momma love,

I don't know when this is going to get to you but I just had to tell somebody. The reason I don't tell Joanie or Sara yet is that I don't know really what's going to happen, and they might make fun of me or something, but I have to tell you.

There were these two fellows that came out here to see Marc about something, on a cycle but they weren't like the ones that came out before. They had just come into town. One of them was older, nearly as old as Marc I think, and his name was Tex. He seemed very nice when he talked to me.

Ben (he's the other one) is past twenty but he wouldn't tell me what his age is exactly. He's nearly six feet tall and just so beautiful. His skin is like bronze or something, and his body is like a statue.

Oops, I guess maybe I just told you. Well, it happened, and it was just perfect. Ben was a little scared I think when he found out I hadn't been with anyone else, and I know he wouldn't have done anything if I hadn't let him. I always thought it would be with somebody I knew for a long time, or really well at least, but with Ben it was just like it was meant to be. Like something that had to happen. Ben tried to pretend he wasn't worried but I know he was.

I really love him a lot, and I miss him. He had to go away with Tex but he said he'd be back as soon as he could. I wish you could meet him. He tries to act rough and mean sometimes like those other bikers, but he's not like that at all. He really loves me, I know he does.

I wish you could meet him, maybe someday you can if things work out.

I'm running out of space so must close. Please don't worry about me. I'm happier than I've ever been before in my whole life. Love and Peace

JILL

P.S. I didn't tell Marc yet. I wonder if he'll be mad?

LIII

tun: retreat

Getting Hot John out of DenPeb had been one thing, and as such, an elementary operation; simpler than they had had any right to hope or expect.

Getting out of the area in one piece was something else again.

For over a dozen hours there had been no trouble; with some effort they had been able to jockey the BMW up onto the braces mounted on the Land Rover's rear end—and that done, they could take to rough country. It would be difficult enough avoiding the GEMs, which could traverse land, mud or water on a cushion of air; if it had been necessary to contend with the Patrol buses as well, things could have become too difficult to handle.

Strategies:

Stay off the roads—avoid the buses and other standard-wheel vehicles.

Try to pick a route involving hills with a better than thirty percent grade—in this situation, a Gem's lack of wheel friction worked against it, making it extremely difficult to control.

Move, under these conditions, only during the hottest part of the day—to confuse the brain guiding the multipointed swords that hang ever above; it cannot differentiate the heat/reflected-light emission of your vehicle finely enough to fling down its furies.

Don't draw any arrows—take an escape route at ninety degrees from your final destination; you have all the time in the world, so remember to take it.

In case of a confrontation, unless your first shot will be the whole match, prime target is the comm rig; there's little point in snuffing your opponent if he's only the front rank of a radio-summoned army.

Don't try for assistance from other outlanders—CenterForce knows them too, and they'll be the first to be checked. Rely on what you can steal or extort from urbos.

Ben was behind the wheel of the Rover now—after so long on a cycle he tended to aim, rather than drive, the vehicle—and Hot John was navigator; behind them, Tex sat at the rear-mounted machinegun, the muzzle of which poked out through a window in the reinforced plating.

They had stopped, now, in middle afternoon, at the edge of a stream bed which still cradled a meager trickle. Ben checked the radiator, then undogged the reserve water can and began to fill it. "What's our position?"

Hot John scowled at the map. "That was two-eighty-seven we passed back there," he said, gesturing. "We're about fourteen miles southest of Kit Carson, if that tells you anything."

Tex looked up from the ammo belt he had been checking. "*Kit Carson*? Are you shitting us? The person or the town?"

"Town. Says so right here on the map. 'Sides, couldn't shit you boys. You're too big of turds."

Ben grunted. "All the old lines, hey? 'Saved your life today, killed a shit-eating dog'—Christ, we should've left you in that place."

"Wow, man. I still don't know why you didn't."

"Because we're fucking idiots, man," said Tex, "and we know good and well that if we'd been in there and you'd been out here you would have been just as much of an idiot as we are. Also I wanted to see if I was still good with a mortar."

"You'd been any better," said Ben, "and you

would've hit those towers so perfect they just woulda met in the middle and wouldn't've blocked the gate."

"Please, my man. I'm a perfectionist. You know, though, that place isn't nearly as rough a proposition as I thought it'd be. About thirty guys, three fieldpieces, a few mortars—" His eyes began to take on the faraway look of a man with a pleasant vision.

Ben shook his head. "Yeah. We'd wipe them out and somebody else would wipe *us* out. Some people tried that once, at the IC near Charleston. Place was closed for a few months, opened up again, and all that had happened was there were a lot more dead or messed-up people around. And they had a lot better combat situation than we've got out here."

"But out here there's the supply problem—oh, fuck it; it was just a thought. Hey, pathfinder, where do we go from here?"

Hot John looked at the map again as Ben dogged down the water jug. "Due south should do it," he said finally. "Into the Panhandle and then cut back—"

crackle   hiss

"Sweepbeam!" yelled Tex. "Coming this way!" Even as he said the last word Ben had the Rover in gear. The vehicle lurched forward, as behind it a yard-wide swath of scrub turned black, then gray, becoming ashes without experiencing flame.

As the Rover rolled over the rise of the stream bank they could just make it out, far back on the highway; similar to a standard Patrol bus except for the pyramid-stacking of pipes along the full length of its roof, and parabolic reflectors at each end.

"You do anything?" Ben shouted to Tex.

Tex grimaced. "Not at this range. But they were lucky, damn lucky. Those things got the range you can knock down a satellite with them if you focus them right, but you got to aim them just like anything else. They only got near us because the way that stream runs happened to give them line-of-sight. Soon's you get over this thing—there. We can relax for a few seconds."

"Still want to take the south route?" asked Hot John.

"It's as good as anything," said Ben. "Besides, the last they could see us we were still heading east. For all they know we still are."

Hot John nodded. "Right. They probably already have somebody heading up—three-eighty-five, it is—to meet us."

"Well," said Tex as he resecured the machinegun, "he gonna have him a long wait."

"Don't feel too sorry for him yet," said Ben. "The day is three hours to being over, plenty of time for all kinds of fun and games."

"You have to look on the bright side, my boy."

Ben grinned. "Wasn't I?"

LIV

pi: holding together

We're not rugged individualists and we're not loners.

StarChild isn't a camp where people stay while they're waiting to go back to the cities, and it isn't an aid station for warriors and barbarians—or whatever they want to call themselves.

What we are is a *community*—in the same sense, maybe, as the town you grew up in—maybe not as large, maybe without a lot of the conveniences you had there; but a community.

Being somewhat newer than most communities, Star-Child has to face a lot of problems that can't be solved by one person, or two, but by every one of us, working together. And the problems of the community have to come first.

To a lot of you the above may sound as though I'm belaboring the obvious, but unfortunately that hasn't been the case. We know, from our own experience and what we've heard from other places like this, that a lot of you come out here without really dropping the urbo way of life and taking up a new way.

And what's the new way?

It could be as simple a thing as picking up a piece of paper from the ground; or noticing that the wood supply is down and getting some more; or watching the goats when you see there's no one else around at the moment.

If you live here, you can't ever use the phrase 'that's not my responsibility.'

If you live here, *everything that happens here* is your

responsibility—since everything here is yours, as much as anyone else's. Just loving thy neighbor isn't enough; you have to help your neighbor, as your neighbor will help you.

That, in short, is what makes StarChild—and the places like it—*different* from the town you grew up in.

And that's why we'll be here, long after those towns and cities have choked to death—choked on hate and indifference.

> —Marc Hammond, *StarChild Bulletin*
> *Number Ninety-three*: Community

LV

po: splitting apart

. . . but why should such things surprise me, at this late date? Surely there is no new thing in the pattern of love and hate, of birth and death, of affection and lust—is there?

Yet when I look at young Marriette Gaines—when I see what was done to her in the name of a sick hunger, far beyond mere sexual passion—I must admit that I am as far from understanding humanity as ever I was.

What path did she take, to bring her now to a bed where she hovers on the very edge of mortality, while beyond the door waits a father who rages at her so that one would think she was the perpetrator of this terrible thing rather than the victim?

So easy to call upon the parlor psychology, to see in Edward Gaines' fury an uncontrollable jealousy of the unknown person who deprived him of that which he could never admit to wanting; to see one whose unbidden desires while his wife was still alive became haunting whips of guilt after her death.

So easy, this psychology—but the philosophical difficulties are not as easily dismissed; what of the victim? Again, what brought her to this evil pass? Shall, in fact, the sins of the father be visited upon the daughter?

It would seem so. As I write, Gaines rages about the town, filled and glowing with the promise of more pain and suffering; if it should happen that he finds the target he seeks, and does not destroy it utterly, will he understand that I must try as hard to save the life of that victim as I do with this present one? I doubt it.

Gaines waits only for the accusing words from his daughter; her whisper or whim may well be a death sentence for some random wanderer. From what little I have learned of her, and the far too much I know of her father, I can but wonder: will she tell him anything, anything at all?

—from the daily journal of
Dr. M. J. Michelson
(all dates deleted)

LVI

fu: return

This time it was not Grogan, with his fun and games; this time the bullet sped past his ear with a vicious cracksnap of rending air.

They had crossed the breadth of New Mexico and traveled well into Arizona; when they intersected 164, a state road which did not appear to have been used for weeks, the BMW was offloaded. They would take their separate paths to Marble Fork—the path of the Rover almost straight due west, but with many bumps, lurches and changes in altitude; that of the BMW much more roundabout, and much smoother.

Clean highway; covered with dust, but no rubble and few cracks. The occasional abandoned car or truck; once, the wrecked and burnt hulk of a Center-Force Patroller. Ben set a cruising speed of mile-per-minute, and thought about Jill.

What, and no joke, what was he getting himself into? It had been nice, nice like he hadn't believed it could be, and she hadn't been like those other girls. What was it? Yeah. She had mattered, it was that simple. Those other ones—all right, just a way to pass the time, but they hadn't really been people, not like her. Maybe because she had been a virgin?

No; it seemed like it had started before that, when he first saw her. She was—she was just *different*, and that was it.

So what was he going to do about her, about his little *novia*? (She had liked that word.) He hadn't

really been planning to do much in Marble Fork—
except bang Trina, and now that seemed like a waste of
time, more trouble than it was worth. Hell, he hadn't
planned at all; there hadn't seemed to be much point
in trying to figure angles for the future. So?

She was hung up on him, but they always got that
way if you were the first; she'd get over it if he went
away. If? Well, of course he was going away; couldn't
stay here for the rest of his life, and he couldn't very
well take her with him. She wouldn't last a minute, not
a little one like her. So what could he do? He wasn't
going to give up the rest of his life, hell, even for this
princess . . .

. . . what could he do in Marble Fork, anyway? From
what he'd heard, that cat Chino was set up for the
second spot, and Ben would have to deal him one way
or the other to take his place in that slot—and that was
if Grogan wanted him around for any length of time
anyway; Ben had the feeling he didn't.

What else was there to do, a town like that? Just
wouldn't work, man, shit, no way.

Into the town: not quite into the path of the bullet.

Ben hit the ground rolling. Two more shots, mark-
ing the direction of his path, and the ricochet whine,
stopping suddenly. A voice.

Gaines' voice. "Kill you, you bastard! I'll blow your
fuckin' guts out!" Another shot, ripping through the
post beside Ben's head. The Winchester, still in its
holster on the downed cycle; not good. The shot had
come from that walkway between the bar and the hard-
ware store. If he could . . .

. . . he hadn't seen the fist; it must have been an
awfully fast punch, left shoulder, he was spinning and
something hit his knees . . . the ground? Someone had
poured soup or something down his back, damnit,
warm and wet . . .

Ben could turn his head (sand-grit on the mouth) and
see across the street, but it was getting to be night or

dark very quickly. Someone was lying on the ground over there; was it a reflection? No, there were two other people standing there, and there weren't any here.

It got very dark and hard to hear things, too—maybe the darkness was thick like a blanket—but he heard:

"Gaines. Flipped out, I clouted him one. I think he snuffed that one in the driveway. Michelson better . . ."

Ben couldn't hear any more; trying to think was like trying to thread a needle with your eyebrows dripping sweat. Slipping from him, now; who was talking?

Chino?

LVII

ta yu: possession in great measure

INTERNATIONAL MEDIA SERVICES
TR1045AM CST
(DATE DELETED)
ST. LOUIS, MO.
  A SPOKESMAN FOR CENTERFORCE HEAD-
QUARTERS HERE ANNOUNCED TODAY THAT
PERSONS RESPONSIBLE FOR THE RECENT
ATTACK ON THE DENPEB DETENTION IN-
STALLATION HAVE BEEN KILLED IN A SHOOT-
OUT CONFRONTATION WITH PURSUING OFFI-
CERS.
  TWELVE PERSONS, ALL WHITE AMERICAN
MALES, WERE INVOLVED IN THE UNSUCCESS-
FUL ATTEMPT TO FREE DETAINEES CUR-
RENTLY IN CUSTODY AT THE CENTER.
  ACCORDING TO A CENTERFORCE PRESS
RELEASE, LESS THAN EIGHT HOURS AFTER
THE ATTACK THE WOULD-BE INSURRECTION-
ISTS WERE CORNERED IN A HILLY AREA
SOME MILES WEST OF DENVER.
  IN RESPONSE TO A REQUEST TO SUR-
RENDER, THE MEMBERS OF THE GROUP
FIRED UPON OFFICERS WITH AUTOMATIC
WEAPONS AND A RECOILLESS RIFLE. AFTER
A FORTY-MINUTE EXCHANGE OF GUNFIRE,
RESULTING IN THE WOUNDING OF TWO CEN-

TERFORCE OFFICERS, IT WAS DECIDED TO
EMPLOY THE RECENTLY INSTALLED STS
(SURFACE-TO-SURFACE) MISSILE CAPABILITY
OF THE PATROL BUSES.

ONE MISSILE WAS LAUNCHED, AND SUB-
SEQUENT TO ITS DETONATION AT THE TAR-
GET POINT ALL HOSTILE GUNFIRE CEASED.
CLOSING IN, OFFICERS DISCOVERED THE RE-
MAINS OF THE DOZEN MEN: THERE WERE
NO SURVIVORS.

CENTERFORCE LAB AUTOPSIES INDICATED
THAT MOST, IF NOT ALL, OF THE ILL-FATED
GROUP WERE UNDER THE INFLUENCE OF
NARCOTICS AND/OR HALLUCINOGENS. ALL
BODIES WHICH COULD BE IDENTIFIED WERE
THOSE OF PERSONS LISTED AS FUGITIVES
UNDER PROVISIONS OF THE DOMESTIC EN-
EMIES ACT.

THE CENTERFORCE SPOKESMAN RE-
VEALED THAT THEIR HEADQUARTERS
OFFICE HAD RECEIVED A TELEMEMO FROM
THE CHIEF EXECUTIVE COMMENDING THEM
ON QUOTE THE EFFICIENCY AND DISPATCH
WITH WHICH YOUR HEROIC OFFICERS RE-
SPOND TO THOSE WHO WOULD DESTROY OUR
AMERICAN WAY OF LIFE. THE DEDICATED
STAFF OF CENTERFORCE IS A STRONG BUL-
WARK PROTECTING US FROM THE DERANGED
VIOLENCE OF A MISGUIDED MINORITY END
QUOTE.

A PREVIOUS BULLETIN FROM THE DETEN-
TION CENTER HAD STATED THAT SEVERAL
DETAINEES WERE INJURED IN THE ESCAPE
ATTEMPT. LATEST REPORTS ARE THAT NO
FATALITIES HAVE OCCURRED AND THAT
ONLY ONE DETAINEE REMAINS ON THE
CRITICAL LIST. NO DECISION HAS YET BEEN
MADE AS TO DISCIPLINARY ACTION FOR

THOSE INVOLVED IN THE ABORTIVE BREAK-
OUT TRY.
END TEXT
FOR IMMEDIATE USE   GENERAL
REF1110PM (DATE DELETED)

LVIII

hsiao kuo: preponderance of the small

A phantom-land all her own, a separate universe through which she moved: bordered by the demarcations of pain, a time-space continuum defined by broken memories of brute force and indifferent malice.

This was a dark, shadowy universe; though at times, perhaps as a function of a cyclic law she could not apprehend, it would lighten, become gray-white and transparent like gauze. When this happened she would see Dr. Michelson sometimes, and he would look at her carefully; his lips would move and she thought he might be saying *Marriette* but she wasn't sure and she couldn't understand the other sounds he was making.

Other times she tried to talk to him but it didn't seem as though he could understand her either; it might be because she was talking the language of her private world, a language that (*of course*) only she could know.

Then it would get dark again, as something drew her back into her unique and solitary universe.

Something hurt, something down in the center of her; a cold/hot metal bar, thornpointed, that expanded and contracted with the beating of her heart. Other parts of her—shoulders, legs, neck—felt small but very heavy weights resting on them. Sweaty, sticky-dirty, thirsty; why should she be this uncomfortable in her very own world?

From time to time, in the darkness, the memory would ripple and flicker, like bad reception on a 3V set. The road, the sound of their approach in the twilight . . . stopping; did she know them? . . . the sequence of annoyance/anger/fear/pain/rage/pain/ fear . . . walking, hurting, into the Arizona darkness and into her own . . .

. . . never clear, the images; simultaneously she could remember what had happened and be unable to figure out what had happened.

Darkness graying into light; the room was empty. She thought she made sounds but she was not sure, and after what seemed like a very long time no one had come. The bedcovers were heavy, unbearably heavy; she pushed them away and sat up on the edge of the bed.

Suddenly the spiked metal bar within her grew large and very warm and very heavy. It pulled at her, down and away from the bed; she was too weak to fight against it. It would hurt when she struck the floor, she thought vaguely, but strangely she felt herself relaxing.

Into cool, pleasant wind: she fell and fell, and no floor rose up to meet her.

LIX

sheng: pushing upward

(*Eddy's bar—but not as we have seen it before. Now the chairs and tables have been rearranged to face the bar, and there are no drinks on the tables. The Wurlitzer jukebox is in its accustomed niche, but is silent and dark. It is evening.*

The bar is crowded; there are a number of standees. Grogan is here, with Trina and a number of his cyclists; Ben, wearing an impressive shoulder bandage; Tex; Hot John; Dr. Michelson and Marc Hammond, both obviously feeling ill at ease and out of place; the biker here to be identified as Chino—and the focus of all this, Eddy Gaines, seated in a central position in a chair to which his legs have been tied.

Grogan is seated on a high stool behind the bar, giving the effect of presiding over some sort of court— which, in fact, he is.)

GAINES: This whole thing is stupid. You people don't have any authority to pull this.

GROGAN: Listen, mother, it was just up to me you'd already of been wasted good and proper. If I was you I'd keep my fucking mouth shut.

(*turns to the others*)

If we're gonna do this thing, who's first?

CHINO: Michelson.

GROGAN: Yeah, alright, Doc, get your ass up here. What happened with Marriette before she died, she say who did it?

DR. MICHELSON: Miss Gaines—ah—never regained

full waking consciousness. She opened her eyes and tried to speak at five or six different times, but could only utter meaningless sounds.

GROGAN: Couldn't she remember anything? What'd she die of?

DR. MICHELSON: It is possible that she had some form of what would be called traumatic antero-grade amnesia, but it may also be that one of the concussive blows to the skull caused damage to the speech organization centers. As to the other question, ultimate cause of death was a burst blood vessel and internal bleeding.

CHINO: But she never said anything you could understand.

DR. MICHELSON: No.

GAINES: It was *you* motherfuckers that killed her!

GROGAN: Just one more word, man. That's all it takes, and we just skip this whole fair-trial trip.

(*to Dr. Michelson*)

I guess that's it. Go sit down but don't leave. Who else?

TEX: I'd like to say something.

(*Grogan nods.*)

Whoever it was it couldn't have been Ben. We—John and me—left him the same afternoon you said this thing happened. Unless he can go five hundred miles an hour on that bike there's just no way he could have got here. No *way*.

CHINO: Is that right, John?

HOT JOHN: Just as my man here says.

CHINO: Hammond? What you got to contribute to this feast of reason?

MARC: I'm not really sure. Jimmie said she went out the gate a little before seven when the rest of us were having supper, and that's the last any of us saw of her.

(*hesitates*)

I guess I should say that I don't think that Reed

had anything to do with what happened to Marriette. He and this fellow Tex came out to Star-
Child to ask me some things about the DenPeb
camp, and he just didn't seem like somebody who
would do that. Also—one of the girls seems to
have gotten to know him pretty well, and for
whatever it's worth she doesn't think he could do
a thing like that either.

(*A few people turn to look at Ben, who stays dead-
pan.*)

GROGAN: (*to Gaines*) What gave you the idea that
Ben here had anything to do with it?

GAINES: Well, he'd come into town out of nowhere,
and he went out to that camp where Marriette
was staying with those freaks, and then he goes
away, and this thing happens to her, and then he
shows up again.

CHINO: And on that basis you tried to snuff him? Why
not Tex? *He* got back after it happened but before
Ben showed up.

GAINES: I don't know. I just thought it was him, is all.
He looked just like that freak she ran away with
who knocked her up a few years ago.

BEN: Oh, wow, baby. You tried to do *me* in because
you never got that other cat. You're too much.

GROGAN: (*to Ben*) You're the one with the hole in
your shoulder, what do you want to do with him?
We can't put him in jail or somebody'd have to
watch him. What, shoot him, beat the shit out of
him?

BEN: Oh, shit, man—*I* don't know.

GROGAN: It was me, I'd snuff him.

CHINO: It's up to you, Ben. We could always run him
out of town, but—

GAINES: (*to Chino*) Listen, you, you better not let—
   (*At Gaines' first word to him, Chino's hand has gone
to the sheath knife at his belt, though he is not sure
what he will do; suddenly, however, it all becomes un-*

*necessary. There is a whipcrack explosion and Gaines'
head snaps back and forward, a neat hole in his forehead. Several people duck down, but there are no further
shots; after a pause Jimmie pushes through the doors
and walks slowly into the bar, a .22 rifle at his side.*

*Recognizing him, Marc rises with a stunned expres-
sion on his face.*)

MARC: Jimmie. What are you doing here? What's
    going on?

(*Jimmie points at the slumped figure.*)

JIMMIE: She talked to me. She never talked to any-
    body else much, but she talked some to me. He
    killed her.

(*Chino takes the rifle from Jimmie, who does not appear to notice.*)

GROGAN: What the fuck are you talking about? You
    telling us he raped his own kid?

JIMMIE: No. But it was his fault, it was because of
    him she died. She wanted to stay there, you know?
    She really liked it at StarChild. But she thought
    maybe people didn't like her because of him, or
    they were afraid her being there would cause
    trouble.

(*He is crying.*)

    And she didn't want to bother anybody. She just
    wanted to just be herself. So she left, because of
    him, and that thing happened to her.

MARC: Jimmie. Jimmie. Don't you realize you've
    killed another human being?

JIMMIE: I don't care. He killed *her*. He hurt people. I
    don't care.

TRINA: (*hard-edged and sarcastic*) It looks like you've
    lost one of your faithful, Hammond. Somebody
    else that's found out that some of the best answers
    come out of a gun.

(*Marc's head whips around and he opens his mouth
to speak—but then he thinks better of it.*)

GROGAN: So what happens now? We go through all
    this shit again with this one?

(*Chino gives the body a nudge. It falls out of the
chair onto the floor; the chair, still tied to the legs,
crashes down on top of it.*)

CHINO: Christ, who cares?

LX

ko: revolution

AGENT: Jonathan Gansell/S14 B2a
LOCATION: Marble Fork, Arizona
DATE: (deleted)
COVER OPERATION/PROCEDURE: (deleted)
REPORT NO.:   54
TEXT: This report will supplement the personal debriefing at your HQ of secondary temporarily assigned this agent.

Present indications are that Eddy (Edward) Gaines did not communicate his suspicions regarding this agent to any other individuals; with his death, therefore, present CO/P is again secure.

No further evidence has come to light to indicate identities of those whose assault on Marriette Gaines resulted in her death. Examination of scene indicates that three took part, all cyclists, one of whom was riding a sport model with an L-shaped gouge in front-wheel tread (see Enclosure #A).

It would appear that the possibility of a rivalry between Terry Grogan and Ben Reed has substantially lessened, due in part to Reed's apparent involvement with a StarChild girl known only as Jill (who apparently is the girl whose attempted rape resulted in the murder by Grogan of the biker called Sonny—see previous reports).

The strain of recent events has considerably affected the already poor health of Dr. Michelson; it is doubtful that he will survive the approaching winter.

Information from overt and covert sources indicates

that Ben Reed and Tex Gernicke planned and executed an attack on the DenPeb IC; a passenger brought back in Gernicke's Land Rover, who is known as Hot John, is said to be a former detainee at that installation.

However, as this information is at variance with that of the official Administration and CenterForce sources, it is therefore presumed to be in error. Accordingly, no attempt was made to prevent the departure of Gernicke and Hot John; their destination is unknown. At present, Reed is believed to be at the StarChild ashram.

Jimmie, the underage male who killed Eddy Gaines, is also at the ashram, under special care; he appears to have suffered a complete mental collapse.

The death of Gaines leaving his place of business without an operator, managership has been assumed jointly by this agent and Trina Gordon.

TRANSMITTAL: CODELEX/COMSAT 22/IAA PRIORITY

LXI

yu: enthusiasm

At first she was a window, then a gateway, to a world he had left behind years ago—a world he had thought, vaguely, no longer existed.

During the day they would work at their tasks, sometimes separately, as often as possible together. In the evening; out in the desert scrub, or in her pie-slice of the dome she shared with Sara, Joan and little Joshua.

Some friends were visiting the girls; laughter, guitars, the incense-sweetness of the pot pipe. Ben and Jill were sprawled on a fungus-like mound of small cushions, drifting with the sounds and the stonedness and the very awareness of each other.

and babe, you got me doing dances
and you got me taking chances
and just acting like a daredevil clown . . .

"Mmf. Weird song," said Ben. "Sounds paranoid."

"You better not let Sara hear you say that."

"Por que?"

"Because," Jill explained, "it was written for *her*, way back when. Some guy that she went through a bad scene with."

Ben listened to the rest of the song. "He write it before the bad scene, or after?"

"Before, I think."

"Yeah. Looks like he was right, then, doesn't it?"

Jill poked at him. "Don't always take the man's side. If he knew all that before then why'd he get into a thing with her?"

Ben pulled her over on top of him. Just before their

lips met, he said, "Maybe he was like me with you. Maybe he just couldn't help himself."

Somewhat less than a quarter of a million miles above them, the moon hung at full. The light it reflected illuminated a scene that could itself be a part of the lunar landscape. The many domes and squat box-like structures, the roughly bleak landscape, the icy clearness—only the patches of desert shrubbery and the drifting sounds of music and laughter broke the illusion of a moon-base.

"Ben?"

"Um?"

"What are we going to do?"

"About what?"

"Us. Are we going to stay here, or what?"

Ben propped himself up on one elbow. "Hadn't really thought about it. I suppose I should."

"It's just that—well, I know you don't mind it here, but it just seems sometimes like maybe we should go someplace by ourselves."

"Any idea where?"

"No."

"Babe, it's just that it's really rough out there, and I'd really worry about taking you with me—no, no, hold it, I didn't mean that like it sounded. It's just that it's pretty bad sometimes, and we have to think about that."

"I don't care how dangerous it is. I'll go wherever you want to go."

"Yeah. Just like Ruth in the Bible. Well, *I* don't want to go getting you shot or something. This place is better than that happening. But you're right, we can't stay here forever. Don't worry about it, I'll figure something out."

They talked for a long time, and could decide nothing, and talked again, through the afternoons and evenings.

They made plans; Jill talked with the others of StarChild and Ben checked with the bikers in Marble Fork; and what they learned would cancel the plans, or diminish them to a small fragment of possibility.

If they had stopped to think about it, neither Jill nor Ben would have been able to explain—to themselves or each other—why it was so important that they plan what would happen with their lives.

They were not yet aware that their instincts were struggling blindly to construct a future for the new life they had created—

—a new life to face a world where the future, like the past, lay in ruins.

LXII

ch'ien: the creative

The will to dominate
    is the will of the narcissist,
    a desire that all things
    shall reflect him.
The love of order
    and regimentation
    finds its seed in the fear
    of a random universe.
The adherence to law
    rather than justice
    is the function of a belief which denies
    the uniqueness of the individual.
Where these three intersect
    a structure of action is formed
    which we call a government.
The primary function of any government
    and the central point of its design
    is to perpetuate itself.
It therefore must control
    those whom it *****
ABNORMAL END
CHECK PROGRAM RUNNING
GENERAL PROGRAM MALFUNCTION
PROGRAM END

    (TRANSLATOR'S NOTE: It was at this point, it
would appear, that the *lin ho* computer ceased running
and printout of its MORAPHIL [rough approximation
of the designation] program. From available informa-

tion, it seems that the combined efforts of programmers and linguistics specialists at the huge Tientsin complex were unsuccessful in reactivating the program. The above fragment must stand as is—the last of the giant computer's "visions.")

—lin ho: *Visions On A Mud Ball*
translated by Chester Valentine

LXIII

tui: the joyous

Momma love,

It's kind of weird to write these letters and not ever know if you get them or not. Maybe Ben will be able to figure out some way you can write to us later.

We're going to go down to Mexico for a while. Ben knows some people down there and how to get us across the border and all that. I guess I should say here that we're going to have a baby! I just found out from the doctor that comes out here. It must have happened that very first time, and I think that means something about how we belong together.

We'll stay down there until after the baby's born and maybe for a while after that, then we might come back up around here. Ben thinks maybe there's a way we could get to Europe or Morocco and we might do that but we don't know yet. If we do maybe there's some way I can see you before we go. I'd really like to see you again. Daddy too.

Ben looked at what I wrote just now and says I should tell you that there's two or three good doctors in this place where we're going so you shouldn't worry about what will happen when I have the baby. We don't know what we're going to call him yet. (Or her, but I really think it's going to be a him—a little tiny Ben!)

I'm going to miss Joanie and Sara and Marc and the other people here, you know, it's the first real home that I've had—a home of my own, I mean. But it will be nice to have a place all to ourselves, and not have to worry about the police coming and taking us away. Love and Peace.

JILL

P.S. I'll write you again as soon as we get down there.

LXIV

chi chi: after completion

(EXTRACT FROM CORRO MANUSCRIPTS/FRAG. 101a)

. . . these, perhaps the most ironically saddening observation regarding the *denouement* was that it was not at all surprising.

The move was not without political precedent; similar programs had been implemented in Russia during the Thirties, Germany during the Forties, and certain areas of Southeast Asia in the Sixties. The Administration was, of course, careful not to draw these historical parallels.

The assassination of a Senator who, curiously enough, had been a sponsor of the ill-fated Amnesty Bill, was the emotional peg on which this expansion of DE Act policies was hung. Theodore North's murder was laid at the doors of various figures in the "insurrectionist" movement; all those identified were fugitives and therefore, of course, unavailable for comment.

Though a news blackout was attempted, it was not an unqualified success; reaction from U.N. Headquarters was sharply critical, and member nations voted unanimously for censure. The United States responded to this with a general denial, coupled with the then-apparently-irrelevant statement that its internal policies were not the concern of the international body.

Among the major Proscribed towns, San Francisco, California, and Atlanta, Georgia, were almost totally destroyed; others were, relatively speaking, more fortunate, in some cases losing less than a fifth of their population before capitulation to government forces.

With the destruction or subjugation of these towns, CenterForce gained considerably more control over major highway networks; rates of capture (or, more often, death) of unauthorized travelers rose steadily.

It is impossible to speculate just how long such a program might have been sustained; in this particular case it must remain an open question. Less than four months after activation of the policy, with a few Proscribed towns still holding out against government forces, total destruction of the national seat of government in New York (along with most of its members and over fifteen square blocks in central Manhattan) was effected by a nuclear device. The bomb was a surface detonation; it is estimated that Ground Zero was located on the terrace just north of the Meeting Hall.

Within hours, four different military juntas had attempted to seize control of the government, but without success; there was simply nothing left to seize. The final outcome of this phase was, as noted above, predictable.

CenterForce Headquarters in St. Louis possessed the only remaining national network of communications, officials—and, most importantly, armed men. Within a month it had established itself as the *de facto* national government, and had gained considerable popular support.

An ironic twist, perhaps, is that the expanded DE Act policies, believed to be the major contributing factor in the sudden ascendancy of CenterForce, were deactivated in the sudden press of reorganization and bureaucratic expansion efforts. Those few remaining Proscribed towns were left as they had been in the past . . .